CW00433815

JANE AUSTEN

AND THE

LONELY LIBRARIAN

MARCUS JAMES

Copyright © Marcus James 2021

All rights reserved. No part of this book may be reproduced or used in any manner without written permission of the copyright owner except for the use of quotations in a book review.

This is a work of fiction. Names, characters, places and incidents are either the product of the author's imagination or are used fictitiously.

Email: marcusjamesinfo@gmail.com
ISBN: 9798517904867

One

An invitation

George Sanders pushed the bolt across the heavy oak door, watched the last rays of the autumn sun dip behind the cathedral and considered the unexpected invitation. He walked slowly up the round staircase, checking the sash windows on each floor. At the second floor he walked across to the far bookcase and pulled out a hardback book from the highest shelf. It was a handsome volume, no doubt, but not extraordinary. Gold and vermilion cover, silk ribbon and silver leaf on the page edges. Gilt lettering on the spine. *Jane Austen. Persuasion.* George took the book to the window and tilted the cover to the last of the light, for the second time that evening. It shone gently. He took an ivory coloured business card from the top pocket of his tweed jacket and replaced it gently in the ribbon-marked page. It said –

Miss Austen requests the pleasure of your company
Midnight Saturday; the library, second floor.
Come and meet Captain Wentworth.

Well, what kind of message was that? A joke, perhaps, by one of their readers. Or by one of his colleagues. Anne could have placed it there. He checked the last sash, glanced around the room and left, clicking off the lights.

Meet Captain Wentworth! A chap dressed up like Captain Wentworth? Why? Okay, he was a Jane Austen enthusiast, but this was odd. *Midnight*! Not very convenient.

By the time he was pedalling slowly down Cathedral Avenue, rattling on the cobble stones, he had made up his mind. He smiled gently like someone leaning into a private joke and slotted his old Claud Butler into the rack with the rather sportier affairs in the apartment bike room. George's place was on the first floor, rented to him by an indulgent godfather whose generosity he blessed every day. His friends found it hard to believe that a thirty-something librarian could afford a large apartment with views across the cathedral greens. He couldn't, of course and only revealed his guilty secret after some months of gently misleading them. Ben and Joe were college friends who dropped by when they could, enjoying the easy camaraderie which is the preserve of old companions. Jules was a fellow librarian and long-standing friend who happened to live three thousand miles away in America. George's godfather Jack suggested secrecy but gave no good reason other than the mischievous instincts of a chap who liked to keep a few jokers up his sleeve. He was the infamous friend of the family, the Jack-made-good through who knew what means. George was just grateful. He made a mug of Earl Grey, settled by the window and considered the time difference to Maine.

Jules Martinez looked at the clock as her phone chimed next to her. That would probably be George. She relaxed back on the sofa, kicked off her sneakers and smoothed her long hair back over her shoulder. Glancing out of the double doors at the fruit trees reflecting the fading light, she was reminded why fall was her favourite season.

"Hey George" she said, picking up the phone.

"Hey sweetie" said her husband Patrick, grinning from the screen. "Not George", he added, redundantly.

"Oh, hey, Pat, where are you?"

"On my way back, we finished early. Are the kids in bed?"

"Fast asleep already, tired out after school."

"Okay sweetie, just heading off, see you in about a half hour."

"Okay". Jules tapped off and sighed. The phone chimed again and she glanced up. This time it was George, his bespectacled avatar face glowing at the screen centre.

"Hey George"

"Hey Jules, time for a quick chat?"

"A half hour for you, but no more, you naughty night owl."

George's face appeared in full screen, lit softly by a

standard lamp. Jules looked admiringly at the rows of oak bookshelves behind him, the volumes neatly arranged.

"How's Maine then Jules, all quiet on the Eastern seaboard?"

"Oh you know, the usual routine. An interesting day at the library though, we had a visit from the governor herself. We showed off the new interactive rooms - the younger readers love the moving holograms and touch screen walls. We had C S Lewis reading from *Voyage of the Dawn Treader*. They thought it was awesome. He was full height, walking around the room, totally convincing."

"It sounds fantastic, we'd love one of your benefactors," said George. "Could you loan us one?"

"Sorry George, you'll need your own tame millionaire."

"Okay, it's always worth asking. At least we have our hologram chess, the students love that. Thank you for The Henry James by the way, it arrived yesterday. I don't know if I can catalogue it - I'd rather take it home and squirrel it away. That embossed etching may be the most beautiful cover I've seen this year."

"Well don't sweat it George, you'll still be able to read it when they're finished with it. So who's the Henry James fan?"

"Oh, that's the lovely Poppy. She's really into nineteenth century Americana. She's got a wicked sense of humour - works locally at a publishing house and comes in to use the old journals. Loves the classic Vogues and the Vanity Fairs. She was here yesterday and showed me a diamond engagement ring her grandmother gave her. She told me that she's still waiting for Mr Right! At least she'll have a Tiffany on her finger for the engagement party."

"Wow, you do get the interesting readers don't you? Everything else okay there? By the way, is that Mozart you're listening to?"

"Yes, Magic Flute. I like Papageno, he's a bundle of fun. It's one of Uncle Jack's old vinyl albums."

"Not one of Emily's?"

"No, not Emily. I don't think she's ever sung in the Magic Flute. You remember the recording when she played Barbarina in Figaro?"

Jules paused, looking out at the trees swaying in the breeze. "Yeah, I still have it, it's beautiful. So, you're not wallowing in it then, just enjoying some Mozart?"

"Absolutely. A bit of Wolfgang Amadeus is just the ticket after a lively day." He glanced across at the gilt-framed photograph of Emily on the sideboard, forced a smile and reached for his tea. "Anyway, there is *something* I would like to chat over with you."

"Go on, I'm intrigued."

"Long story short, I was shelving a vintage copy of *Persuasion*, when I noticed a business card, just peeking out of the top. It said ..." George paused for effect,

"Miss Austen requests the pleasure of your company. Midnight Saturday, the Library. Come and meet Captain Wentworth."

Jules thought for a few seconds. "Hmm."

"Hmm? Is that the best you can do?"

"I'm *thinking*!"

"Okay. Take all the time you need. *So*?"

Jules smiled, apparently playing for time. "Well, the obvious possibilities. A joke, by one of your readers?"

George smiled, "I thought of that too. Then I thought it could be you. *Was* it you? One of your new holograms?"

"Not me! If I wanted to trick you, I'd have thought of something much more fun than making you turn up at midnight, even though you love to stay up all hours."

"So one of our readers or a colleague?"

"Have you upset anyone enough to prank you?"

"Nooo. Well, probably not. Anne has a sense of fun, but she's really not the practical joking kind. I do have the odd quarrel with the Professor, you know, Dobbs. He rarely smiles; told me I was born in the wrong century. Just because I use a fountain pen with green ink! You remember I told you about his scary eyebrows and bushy beard. He chairs the Trustee board and glares at me over his reading glasses. Very liberal with his corrections and suggestions. Sorry, I digress. I can't think of anyone I've rubbed up the wrong way."

"Who had the book out last?"

"It was on loan to a subscription library in Cornwall, came back in the post on Monday."

"One of your gold key holders?"

George thought for a moment. "Possibly. They do have twenty-four-seven access."

"Well, so many possibilities. I guess you'll just have to turn up on Saturday night and see what happens. Captain Wentworth huh? Could be fun!"

"My thoughts exactly." George leant back in his

armchair and reached for his tea. "Shall I call you after?"

Jules laughed. "Yeah, why not."

"How's Patrick and the family?"

"They're good, thanks for asking. Patrick's back in a half hour. Did you catch up with Emily and Jax?"

"Mm, we had hot chocolate and carrot cake in Banks, that new coffee shop down by the Tarn bridge. Emily was fine, before you ask and Jax is great, growing up fast, full of opinions."

"Cool", said Jules, looking serious. "I know it's been a while and I know how … difficult it can be. So don't be all English and keep it in, okay? Talk to me."

"I will, thank you Jules".

"Did you have your new home manager delivered? Ours came last week, but we haven't even set it up yet."

"I installed it but it's not live yet. Not much of a techno geek, as you know."

"You give it a name yet?"

"I tried several and they were all rejected as too common. You'll see, it's not as easy as it sounds."

Jules looked around for inspiration. "So it couldn't handle the name Hal. Or Computer. Or Bob?"

"No, nor could it deal with Dickens, Trollope or Eliot"

"Really? You want to say "hey Trollope" to schedule a haircut?"

"Of course I would! What could be more fun?"

"*George*."

"Oh dear, the look of disapproval. I'll think of something. I seem to be the last in this block to have one. My neighbour Sally is always saying, "George, you have to have a home manager. My *Oola*, I think she said it's called, is brilliant. Guesses what I want to eat, orders it up, arranges the house bots, asks me what I want to watch, tells me off for eating too much chocolate."

Jules looked incredulous. "Really, her home manager watches her diet?"

"You can set it to monitor your weight, calorie intake, even your exercise. The scariest idea I heard though is where it tells you off for daydreaming too much. Suggests some yoga, to make you focus."

"Well, it's all a bit big brother, so I won't be setting it up as a snooping dog."

"Good for you. Convenience only, no snoops." George looked across at the clock. "Well, time to climb the hill to Bedfordshire, I think."

"You don't have stairs".

"Okay, fair point. Thanks for our little chat. I'll let you know how my assignation with Captain Wentworth goes."

"Please do."

"Good night Jules."

"Good night George."

He tapped his phone and stared out at a couple of street lights coming on like glowing pearls as a man walked quickly along the path to the cathedral green. The lights disappeared with his shadow.

George collected the books for shelving and stepped briskly up the stairs to the first floor. There were only ten readers in that day, a quiet Thursday, just a handful of students and Roxie. That was just as well, because his colleague Anne was away for two weeks, visiting her mother in Aberystwyth. Kamal and Raj were sitting at their usual table at the far end of the room, working on their laptops. Raj was a student librarian and happy to work a variety of unsociable hours, to help keep the library open for readers. George knelt down to shelve an oversized Psychology book by Gross and considered the not unreasonable idea that Kamal or Raj could be behind the midnight meeting. Kamal was both clever and creative, in the final year of his Phd in nano-materials and a more than proficient jazz guitar player. George had sat quietly in the corner of *Sylvie's* brasserie in Baker Square last summer, whilst Kamal and a band of college friends ran through lively versions of *Fly me to the Moon* and *My Funny Valentine*. It was a stimulating evening, his first night out for a few weeks and he felt energized after a chat with Kamal and his bandmates.

As George moved down the room, Raj turned in his seat and called across, "hi George, can I ask a question?"

"Fire away" said George, taking a seat opposite them, at the large oak table.

"Where would you look for a hard copy on bioplastics? The university only has ebooks and links to academic papers, nothing real and straightforward that I could use as an introduction, even in the chemistry department, I checked."

"Okay", said George, "we'll have a look at the Share database and the British library, see if we can rustle up a copy."

"Thanks George"

"Pleasure, I'll be back in a tick." He paused. "I don't suppose either of you are Jane Austen fans?"

Both Kamal and Raj looked up at him quizzically. Then Raj smiled and said, "not really a fan, but I do like Pride and Prejudice, we did a production at school. Why, are you starting a book club or something?"

"No, just a little obsession of mine. I'll see you in a minute." He crossed the room to the desk next to the stairs and clicked on the catalogue. A sing-song American voice came across from the window where Roxie was sitting in an armchair with a copy of the Times. "*I'm* a fan, George".

"Of Miss Austen?"

"Yes, I've read them all. Except Sanditon, of course. I wasted quite a few hours on that television production where the writer tried to complete it and made a damn hash of it. It's quite a skill to imitate her style, don't you think?"

"I agree."

"But my favourite is Sense and Sensibility. Such an enchanting film adaptation, by … who was it?"

"Ang Lee. Yes, quite magical, he really captured the passion under the surface I think."

"Oh, yes," said Roxie, relaxing back into the armchair and looking as if she were entranced by the memory, "the actor who played Edward …"

"Hugh Grant."

"That's the fellow. My father used to meet men like that in Nassau, strolling around the harbour like they were in Kensington Park. The sea seemed to glow you know, the sand, so, so white, we would eat conch salad at the harbour side and watch the world go slowly by." Roxie seemed to drift off into reminiscence.

"So, Roxie," asked George, "are you using Jane Austen in your work at all?"

"My history piece? Not really, just by reference to her brothers, who were in the Navy. They did pretty well, didn't they?"

"Certainly, top of the tree. One became an Admiral."

"Wow." Roxie closed her eyes for a moment and George wondered if she were picturing herself on a British frigate pursuing Captain Blackbeard across the bay.

"For the record, my favourite novel is Emma," said George. "It's perfect."

Roxie opened her eyes again and sat up. "Good choice," she said and picked up her newspaper, as if to bookend the conversation.

George decided that Roxie was not in the running for mystery writer and marvelled once again at the way people attached themselves so personally to their favourite authors, even one chronicling society more than two centuries ago. He went back to the catalogue desk to continue his bioplastics research for Raj.

From: Jules Martinez
To: George Sanders

Hey George

Just a couple of updates …

Mrs Russell, you know, the new boss, called me into her glass office this morning and told me she won't be around for a few weeks. Just said she has to take care of some personal business. She's such a funny creature, never finishes a sentence, just throws out half orders and then trips out the room to another meeting, leaving me standing there. So, a few more late nights for me anyway.

I had a box of half price architecture books from Fred, the bookstore guy I told you about. He's decided to move south and start afresh selling vitamins on the net. Good luck Fred! I've taken pity on you poor Brits and packed you up some books by the two Franks, Lloyd Wright and Gehry, you know, the guy who designed the Museum of Pop Art? I think you'll like them.

One other thing. You know that card invitation you found in the copy of Persuasion?

I had one too!

Two

Persuasion

... there could have been no two hearts so open, no tastes so similar, no feelings so in unison, no countenances so beloved. Now they were as strangers; nay, worse than strangers, for they could never become acquainted. It was a perpetual estrangement.

George sat in the old leather armchair facing the window, feeling rather foolish. He tried to tame his unruly hair, took off his tortoise-shell glasses and gave them a clean. What was he thinking, sat there at nearly midnight, waiting to meet Captain Wentworth? He replaced his glasses, then looked around the second floor once more, to see if anything had changed since this afternoon when he closed up. There was nothing. He took a sip of water from his glass and waited.

At midnight exactly, he jumped in his chair. The

bells! Of course, the cathedral bells, chiming the hour. Not twelve bongs like Big Ben, just the hour chime. He relaxed a little, staring out at the gothic tower in the muted lights around the courtyard. After another minute, he noticed a rose colour growing in intensity in front of the bookcase to his left, where he had found the invitation card three days earlier. He turned to face the light and saw to his astonishment a figure appear, becoming more three-dimensional by the second. A moment later, a full-height woman stood two metres from where he sat, dressed in an autumn pelisse in azure blue, with a white bonnet. He looked more closely at the face and its gentle expression. There was no doubt. It was Jane Austen.

George stood up slowly and walked towards the figure. Before he could reach out to touch her, she spoke:

"Do sit down George."

Feeling even more foolish, he stepped back to his armchair, keeping his eyes on her. The voice was light, considered, firm.

"Underneath your chair, you will find a small package. Please unwrap it. You will find some glasses and gloves. Put them on and follow the instructions."

"Okay," said George, hesitantly, feeling under his seat where there was indeed a paper packet, taped to the underside. He opened it to reveal a pair of visor-like blue-tinted glasses and what he recognised as haptic virtual reality gloves. "So, you're a hologram, is that right?"

The figure paused for a second and replied: "that is

a reasonable question. I am, however, disinclined to answer it at present."

"Right, fair enough." George pulled on the haptic gloves and replaced his own glasses with the blue-tinted ones, which extended down over his ears. They wrapped around his eyes comfortably. "May I call you Jane?"

"You may call me Miss Austen."

"Fine, Miss Austen it is then."

Looking ahead, George could see a white screen. It filled his vision as if he were sitting in the front row of a cinema. Words started to appear, scrolling across the screen.

Welcome George. You are about to enter the novel Persuasion, by Jane Austen. By continuing your journey, you agree to the terms and conditions of the Knightley Corporation. You have one hour to complete your quest. Solve the clues and exit by the green door. If you wish to end the quest early, say exit and you will find a door. If you remove the glasses at any time, please close your eyes for ten seconds, to adjust to normal light. We hope that you enjoy your adventure. Point ahead to proceed.

George removed the glasses and looked across at the figure.

"Sorry Miss Austen" he said, "but why me?"

The figure paused. "Why not?"

"And Jules? Can anyone play this game?"

"Did I say that it was a game? Only you and Jules

are chosen at present."

George felt slightly irritated by the enigmatic answers, but decided to play along. He didn't want to disappoint Jules, who he was sure would be having fun and not asking silly questions.

He thought for a moment and then said: "is there anything else I need to know? Is there a prize?"

Again, there was a pause.

"Enlightenment," said Miss Austen and her whole figure disappeared, leaving George wondering if she had been there at all.

George shrugged, rather impressed by the performance and theatricality of it all. He raised his right hand and pointed. The white screen dissolved, to reveal a wide beach and an azure blue sky. The sound of laughing seagulls and gently breaking waves sounded in his ears. He was standing on the sand, about a hundred yards from the sea. He turned his head to the right and his view moved seamlessly around the beach to a small harbour. He turned gently left and saw the curved bay unfolding, revealing distant duned hills and on the far left, a variety of stone town buildings and a clock tower.

He looked at his hands and down at his legs. He was dressed in a plain brown coat, unbuttoned, with blue trousers and long black leather boots. He could see a yellow embroidered waistcoat and feel a soft silk cravat. A firm forward wave of his hands moved his character. He pointed ahead and moved forwards at a steady pace. The reality of the surroundings was extraordinary, the feeling in his hands quite unlike any virtual reality he had experienced before. Walking right, he could see a trio of fishing boats enjoying the modest swell. The stone harbour wall stretched far out to into the bay. He recognized it at once. That was the Cobb and this was Lyme Regis! There were grey stone and brick harbour buildings and a handful of people walking along the promenade. He now had his back to the sea and he stood for a full minute, admiring the scene.

He heard a call somewhere off to his right, "George, over here!" A figure was walking towards him, waving. Dressed in an elegant white silk dress and an emerald jacket, there was Jules, her shiny dark hair dancing on the sea breeze.

"Nice hat!" she shouted and George reached up to remove a short top hat. "At your service ma'am" he said tipping the hat. "Funny, I didn't know I was wearing one. Where's your bonnet?"

Jules laughed. "Who knows, who cares! Isn't this is amazing? Have you ever seen anything like it?"

"No, nothing at all. The feeling is extraordinary, I can sense the wind on my hands, the warmth of the sun and all these textures."

"Let's explore," said Jules, "we only have an hour."

"And the clues," said George.

"Oh, sure, but let's take a look around first, okay? Over there"

Jules pointed to the promenade and they walked to the steps. An elderly couple were walking slowly away from them. To their left they could see two small groups of elegantly dressed men and women strolling towards the top of the Cobb.

"Bet you dollars to doughnuts that's Captain Wentworth up there" said Jules.

"The Cobb it is then!"

George tried out the different ways of moving his character along the promenade. A waving motion increased walking speed and they were soon moving along at a decent clip. "So did you have a Jane Austen hologram?" asked George?

"Yeah, she was pretty unhelpful though, I must say. I asked her a couple of questions and all she could say was "thank you for your enquiry, I am unable to answer your question at present" in her plummy English accent. It was great though, even better than the library holograms, more kind of solid looking."

"Is there anyone there with you in the library?"

"No, just the security guard downstairs. I told Patrick we were doing a Jane Austen theme evening. Pretty cool huh?"

"Well I suppose that's what this is, after all," said George. "Except that all the guests are avatars!"

"Wow, check out those hats!" shouted Jules and moved closer to the nearest shop front. It was a milliner's shop with a fine display of lace bonnets. They stood and admired a silk over straw ivory hat which caught Jules' eye. As they stood there, pointing at the bonnets and admiring the details, a man stepped up to the window. He turned to them. He had grey whiskers covering much of his face and a plain black jacket and hat, the only colour a plum waistcoat. The man looked straight at George and reached out a small calling card, similar to the original invitation card. He then turned on his heel and marched quickly away. George held out the ivory card so that he and Jules could both read it. It said:

My first is mad, bad and dangerous to know.
My second shares a name with Anne's father
My third chimes with a silver sound at eleven

Jules took George's hand and led them to a white painted seat at the edge of the promenade, looking out across the bay. She lowered her hand and their characters sat side by side. "I could have used some time to look around, you know. They cut straight to the chase didn't they?"

"Well, it's their party I suppose. We have plenty of time."

They studied the card for a minute.

"Okay," said George, "the first is fairly clear, I'm not sure about the other two."

Jules looked again. "That's Lord Byron right? Mad and bad."

"Absolutely" said George. "So we're talking about poets in the novel Persuasion?"

"Makes sense. Last time I read it was a few years ago, so I don't remember that much. You?"

"A year or so, I think, and I've seen a bbc version recently."

"Anne's an Elliot isn't she, her father is Sir something. What's his name?"

"Sir Walter Elliot, a baronet no less. I think Miss Austen calls him the vainest man in England, or something like that."

"So we have Lord Byron and somebody Eliot. Or Walter somebody. It's a little early for *T.S.* Eliot. How about Sir Walter something?"

"Raleigh?" suggested George. "not sure if he wrote poetry."

Jules laughed and turned to look at him. "You know, you look pretty dapper in that outfit. That bit of grey in your hair, the cravat, the top hat makes you look even taller, and those boots! I would call you, let's see, distinguished!"

George smiled. "Thank you my dear, you look rather charming yourself." He paused, looking out to sea. "I still can't quite believe this, why do you think we're allowed to come? Some kind of test, are we guinea pigs do you think?"

"I really don't know … let's try and enjoy it since we're here and we're the chosen two!"

They were quiet for a minute before George seemed to shake himself out of a daydream.

"Right, okay, concentrate. So which poets are discussed in Persuasion? I remember the scene, Anne Elliot and Captain Benwick. I think they're at the Inn, with Captain Harville, Wentworth and the rest of the party."

"Mm", said Jules, "I remember that poor Captain Benwick had lost his girlfriend or fiancée and young Anne was offering him some reading advice to help him over his sadness."

"Exactly." George thought again, taking off his hat and studying it. "Great Scott!" he said, after a moment,

"Sir Walter Scott!"

"Excellent!" said Jules, "that's two for two. We just need the other one."

"Hmm, well, I can't remember that at all. Silver chimes at eleven. Nope, not ringing any bells, if you'll excuse the pun!"

Jules tapped him on the hand and smiled. "Let's just walk anyway. We haven't met Captain Wentworth yet."

"Or Captain Benwick! We can ask him about the chimes!"

"So we can." She pointed over to the stone steps up to the Cobb.

"George, are we going to need a cover or something? You remember the vicar and Mr Darcy in Pride and Prejudice. They haven't been introduced and Mr Collins goes straight up to Mr Darcy and talks to him and Elizabeth is horrified."

"Ah yes, those Georgian manners. Let's just make something up. Wing it, you know."

"Okay George, not really your style. I guess you can do the talking then!"

They climbed the steps and surveyed the scene. The first group of people had walked away from the Cobb towards the chandler's shops at the quayside. A second, larger group of ladies and gentlemen was walking from the upper Cobb towards the steps to the lower.

"I think that must be Wentworth" said Jules, pointing at the tallest man, who was walking next to a pretty blonde girl of around twenty, her red cape and bonnet fluttering in the wind.

"Yes, Wentworth and Louisa, Anne and Benwick and the Musgroves, that must be them!"

George and Jules climbed the steps to the upper Cobb, felt the strength of the sea breeze and walked to within ten paces of the group. "Let's listen in," said Jules.

"The wind is too great, let us move to the lower walk," said Captain Wentworth. He moved down the stone steps and looked back for Louisa. "Catch me!" she shouted. Wentworth looked cautiously up at her and held out his hands. She stood on the second step and then jumped into his arms. They laughed and straight away Louisa ran up the steps to be jumped down again.

"No!" said Captain Wentworth, "I will not allow it."

"But I am determined that I will," said Louisa and climbed to near the top of the steps.

Captain Wentworth started forward as if to catch Louisa again, but George, who was by now within a few paces of the steps shouted "wait, stop!"

"What are you doing?" hissed Jules.

Louisa Musgrove stood stock still and stared back at George.

"Who are these people?" she asked, pointing at George and Jules.

George stepped forward and bowed to Louisa and down to the others in the party in turn.

"My apologies," he said, "unforgivable of me, I know, we have not been introduced. My name is Mr George Roosevelt and this is my wife Jules. My father is Sir Theodore Roosevelt, recently returned from the new world. I meant no harm, only to warn the young lady that the steps are very slippery and it is quite dangerous to attempt to jump from them."

"Thank you sir, I was trying to tell her that myself," shouted Captain Wentworth. "Will you not all come down now so that we may walk in peace?"

Louisa, apparently becalmed, stepped carefully down, followed by the others.

Jules pulled George to one side and whispered. "What are you doing, you just changed the plot!"

George smiled mischievously, "like I said, let's wing it!"

Jules looked rather apprehensive. "Okay, I hope you know what you're doing."

George turned back to Wentworth who held out his hand. "I am Captain Wentworth, pleased to make your acquaintance, and here the Miss Musgroves, Captain Benwick, Miss Elliot, Mr and Mrs Musgrove. We are shortly to return to Uppercross and are taking a last half an hour to walk along the Cobb. My companions are thrilled by the views and the sea air. For myself, I feel quite at home, as a sailor, you understand. And where are you from, Mr Roosevelt?"

"Oh, I have a small estate in Devonshire. Mrs Roosevelt and I are also leaving Lyme Regis today." George felt Jules' hand pressed into his. "As well as enjoying the landscapes, we are also creating a list of poetry which may be elevating for souls in distress."

Benwick and Anne Elliot, who were standing beside them, both looked across with expressions of surprise. Wentworth smiled broadly. "Sir, I have no hesitation in referring you to my friend Miss Anne Elliot. She has been advising us on the very subject, have you not, Anne? And Benwick, you are a great reader of poetry too."

Benwick inclined his head. "I would not say great. I have a decided preference for poetry, that is all. Miss Elliott has been all kindness in suggesting some new reading for me."

George stepped forward. "Well you may be able to help us, for we have a mystery line of poetry which we have been unable to find out. It refers to something which chimes with a silver sound at eleven."

Benwick's face brightened and he glanced at Miss Elliot. "Alexander Pope" she said and looked across at Wentworth, who returned her little smile.

"Yes, Pope, exactly." Benwick seemed enthused and looked out to the waves. He spoke clearly and slowly as if to the sea itself:

"Thrice rung the bell, the slipper knock'd the ground, and the press'd watch return'd a silver sound."

He turned back to the group who were watching him and seemed to return into his quiet self. Anne and Wentworth were both looking at him with evident admiration.

"Thank you sir!" said George. "You have quite answered our question."

"You are most welcome" said Benwick, "poetry is a close friend to me and I have found a thoughtful fellow reader in Miss Elliot." He nodded to Anne.

Wentworth started walking towards the harbour.

"Sadly we must return to our carriage and our journey. Will you walk with us?"

Jules moved closer to Wentworth as the group walked slowly back, the wind whipping their hair and faces.

"I should like to add one more question, if you would indulge me, Captain," she said.

"Certainly, I am quite at my leisure for questions today." His face reflected a quiet amusement.

"Well, this is a matter of love," said Jules.

"Oh, love! What do we know of love?" said Wentworth. "Ask me another, please, for love makes fools of sensible men."

"Then you find that women are not made foolish by love?"

"On the contrary, I find that Cupid is even-handed in his gifts" said Wentworth, apparently warming to his theme.

"And what if one is disappointed in love?" asked Jules. "One may find it hard to move past regret." George noticed that Jules was also animated by the conversation and seemed to be enjoying herself.

"Then one must stick with one's principles, for they are the guide." Wentworth looked at Anne and held her gaze for a second. "In the madness of anger or jealousy, one is inclined to lose sight of the fundamental idea. That a meeting of minds and shared values is uncommon. In short, that enduring love is rare. One must be patient and understanding, however difficult that may be."

The group had reached the end of the Cobb and were

approaching the chandlery and the Red Lion Inn on the corner. Beyond the Cobb they could see the boatyard and the shingle beach stretching away to the distance. Jules gave a brief bow to Captain Wentworth. "Thank you Captain, I see that your opinion accords with my own." Anne stepped forward and addressing George and Jules said, "The Captain seems to have the last word on the subject. We must return to the carriages. Goodbye."

They walked away and George noticed a lively exchange between them, evidently about the bold couple from the new world.

"Awesome", said Jules, "you certainly put the cat amongst the pigeons. I hope you're satisfied? You've just changed the plot of Persuasion. Louisa won't stay in Lyme Regis and the whole plot will unravel!"

"Not necessarily" said George. "Let's see how the story develops."

"How long do we have left?"

"I don't know, I'd estimate a quarter of an hour or so. Just a minute though." He reached his hand to where a waistcoat pocket would be and pinched his fingers. An ornate silver pocket watch with roman numerals appeared in his hand, showing eleven forty-five. "Well, that looks about right for Lyme Regis time I suppose."

"This reality is quite something isn't it?" said Jules. "I mean, how did it give those characters all those different responses, and adapt the scene to the changes. Incredible!"

"I've seen some amazing artificial intelligence

engines, but nothing this seamless. The ones they used for the Mars missions are out of this world!" They both laughed and Jules gave him a tap on the hand. They walked along the beach and tested the limits of the environment. Where the sand met the water, their characters simply stopped moving forwards.

"No wet feet then!" said Jules and they walked back towards the Cobb.

They strolled slowly back along the promenade towards the Red Lion Inn on the corner. As they approached the milliner's shop a man appeared at George's elbow. It was the same man in the black frock coat who had given them the clue. He walked in step with them and asked, "do you have the answers?"

"To the clues, yes?" said George. "The poets are Byron, Sir Walter Scott and Pope."

The man stopped. "That is correct. You may proceed to the next level." He pointed to his right where a rather incongruous-looking green door had appeared, with the word "Exit" over the top. George looked back and the man was gone.

Some yards in front of them, there seemed to be a commotion by the Inn, with Captain Wentworth's party at the centre of it. As they walked forward, they saw a boy in a sailor's cap chewing an apple and seemingly amused by the sight. "What's happening over there?" asked George.

"Silly girl fell over, that's all mister" said the boy. "Twisted her ankle I'd say."

Captain Benwick came running past them, heading for the town. "Fetching help," he shouted, "Miss

Musgrove has turned her ankle."

"Fantastic," said Jules. "It looks like you broke the story and they just fixed it!"

Three

Uncle Jack

George stared at the porridge in the pan and gave it another stir. "Honey or blueberries?" he mused, looking at the selection on the shelf. His dreams and now daydreams were dominated by the Persuasion experience and the conversation with Miss Austen at the end of their hour in Lyme Regis.

The exit door had worked well as a transition between the virtual world and the library. As he had walked through the green door, the glasses had faded gently from white to black. A voice said: "please close your eyes for a few seconds, remove the visor and relax." As George allowed his eyesight to adjust to the lamplight, he saw that Miss Austen had returned.

"Welcome back, George, and congratulations!"

"Congratulations, why?"

"You solved the clue and you have created a brand new version of Persuasion, in which Captain Benwick accompanies Louisa to Uppercross and they fall in love there."

"Oh," said George, "I'm sorry."

"That's quite alright" said Miss Austen. "The new, let's call it the alternative edition, is rather good."

"In that case, you're welcome."

The hint of a smile appeared on her face. "Why did you change the plot and prevent Louisa from falling at the steps?"

George thought for a second. "I think I just wanted to see what would happen. If a change would play out to recreate the original outcome. Or would the story continue and make no sense. I suppose I could have knocked Wentworth's hat off or kissed Louisa. That would have been interesting!"

"You could. Why didn't you?"

"I felt like I wanted to change the dynamic that's all. Not just play it like a game. I've done that before in simulations and the novelty wears off rather quickly. This was quite different though, more, let's see, immersive." He paused. "May I ask, by the way, are you an ignis fatuous? Like Puck or Ariel?"

The figure was silent for what seemed an eternity. Then she said, "No. I am not here to mislead, I am here as a guide."

"So, we can move to the next level. What does that mean?"

"You and Jules solved the clue and may take part in the next story."

"And what if we hadn't found the answers?"

"Then you would have the option to try again."

"And I don't imagine you would tell me who's

running this show, or whatever you'd like to call it?"

"I am the author. That is all you need to know at present." Silence filled the room.

George thought for a moment and stood up. "Right, well thank you for the little adventure, it was most obliging of you. I'll see you … when?"

"Saturday night at the same time. Come and meet the Dashwood sisters. Goodnight George." Then Miss Austen had disappeared.

George turned off the porridge, sprinkled on some blueberries, then shrugged, added honey, sultanas and pumpkins seeds and settled into his favourite armchair by the window, overlooking the green. The morning news started up on the large screen but did not break his reverie for ten minutes until he was interrupted by a new chime and then a voice over the speakers:

"Good morning sir. I am your new house manager, or virtual butler if you prefer. To finish setting up my services, please allow a thirty minute introduction session. Would this evening be convenient?"

"Oh, hello! You're here already. I thought you'd take longer to load up. I suppose this evening would be okay. Let's say 7.30 then?"

"Very good sir. What name would you like to give me?"

"Well I tried a few with the trial version and they didn't work. I've been thinking, would Bertie be okay?"

"Yes sir. Bertie it is. You have chosen the virtual

butler setting. I will be checking your email for you and alerting you to any that need a prompt reply. I have your contacts and diary already. This evening, we can arrange shopping, communications, health services and leisure activities."

"Leisure? You mean films, music, theatre?"

"Yes sir. I can also arrange holidays for you. Would you like a trip to Las Vegas with an evening of line dancing?"

"What? No! That sounds horrible. I think we'll need to spend some time on personal preferences don't you?"

"Yes sir."

"Ah, right, thanks Bertie. So … could you run a search for me now? I'm looking for companies called the Knightley Corporation?"

"Is that UK or world-wide sir?"

"World-wide but recently incorporated, say in the last five years."

George blew on his porridge and mulled over the people he could discuss Jane Austen virtual realities with. The list wasn't long. His friend Joe enjoyed gaming but that was a whole world of armies, quests and turn-of-the-wrist fighting techniques. Not really his area of interest. Only Jules shared his passion for exploring eighteenth and nineteenth century novels. During August, they had spent many hours discussing the Brontë sisters, their Bell aliases, their American relatives and everything in between. George had accumulated a Brontë box of literary memorabilia, including records of walks and postcards from his visit to Haworth with Emily three years earlier. They had rented a windblown stone cottage on the edge of the moors near Thornton-le-Dale and spent a happy long weekend following the Brontë trails like a pair of devoted pilgrims. Jules could trump his Brontë experience though. She was a veteran of two visits to Haworth, a conference in York and a trip to Maryland, chasing memories of the elusive Aunt Jane. She could qualify as a superfan.

"Sir," said Bertie. "There are ten companies registered under that name. The list is on your screen. And your Uncle Jack is on his way down the street."

"Uncle Jack is here?"

"Yes sir, shall I open the door for him?"

"Yes, of course. We'll need to set him up. I haven't told him about you yet."

George quickly tidied the books and plates off the dining table and looked around the sitting room. It was good enough for Uncle Jack. Although Jack owned the place, he really didn't care about the arrangement of rugs and the placement of house plants. The sitting room door opened and a grinning man with a tanned face and cropped grey hair put his head around the door.

"Uncle Jack!" George shouted. "You didn't say you were coming?"

"Didn't know myself until yesterday Georgie. Lovely to see you." Jack shook George firmly by the hand, looked around the sitting room approvingly and sat in George's favourite armchair by the window. "Don't like your house mate much. Said his name was Bertie and asked me if I would like a house introduction."

"Oh, sorry Jack, we can set you up with Bertie later. New virtual house butler. Every home should have one!"

"Pleased to meet you," said Bertie.

"So you finally gave in and joined the new world then George. Not really my bag, bit too old for all that jazz. Still, I guess you young guns have to move with the times."

"One step at a time Jack. I'm the last in the block to have a home manager. It's jolly convenient, but I'm told they still make the odd cock-up."

"Excuse me!" said Bertie.

"Well, it's true, you butlers are not infallible, that's all I'm saying."

George settled into the opposite armchair. "So, where *have* you been Jack? Last I heard you were in Cuba teaching English. You look well."

Jack laughed. "Well, Cuba didn't last long. Actually I've been on the boats for the last three months."

"The boats?"

"Mackerel fishing, out of Newquay harbour."

"Right, of course, I should have guessed."

Jack leaned forward and said quietly, "nobody been asking after me have they?" He stood up and walked to the curtains, sweeping his gaze across the green. He was of average height, but wiry and angular for a man of middle years. He had retained a modified cockney accent despite growing up in leafy Surrey.

"No," said George. "Only the neighbours, out of

politeness, that's all."

"And Emily, Jax, the library? All okay in your world?"

"Long story Jack. I can fill you in after work if that's okay."

"Suits me Georgie. I'm off for a kip. Catch you later."

From: Jules Martinez
To: George Sanders

Hey George

So are you ready for the Dashwoods then? Do you think I'm a Marianne or an Elinor? I guess we may find out. Miss Austen is a tease don't you think?

Okay, enough questions. I've done some digging this end and it's not at all clear who's running the show. But then, I thought, do I really care?

The Saturday night adventure was great fun and I'm wondering if they can keep it going? I mean are they seriously going to run simulation scenes from all six Austen novels, just for us?

Call me when you're free.

Jules x

"Jack, why are we in a cloister?"

"It's peaceful. I could use some peace. So could you Georgie."

Jack and George were walking in the twilight cloisters of the cathedral after a comfortable dinner at *The Gothic* on the green. They had lingered over wild salmon and potato salad with a crisp and grassy Sauvignon blanc and discussed George's father's research. Jack and Arthur went back a long way. School, college, even working together at the *Salut* bistro where Jack won his chef's whites and Arthur won the hand of Clare. They lived now in fairly contented semi-retirement in Salisbury, where Arthur was working his way slowly through a paper on cultural perceptions of time.

After dinner George and Jack had strolled across the green where Jack greeted the rector at a small arched wooden door to the right of the west face. This seemed to be a prior arrangement as the church warden left holding a bottle-shaped brown paper bag and a sheepish grin.

"I thought it was time for a chat," said Jack.

"Oh dear," said George, having considered himself rather fortunate to avoid a mackerel-style grilling over dinner on the subject of Emily.

"Don't worry lad," said Jack, stopping at the west corner to have a closer look at the mullions and gothic tracery. "I'd just like to know where you are? Have you had a proper chat with your mum and dad recently?"

"Yes, please don't concern yourself Jack. We are in communication."

"And yet."

"Yet?"

"It's been a year Georgie - how often do you see

Emily and Jax?

George sighed and leant against a column. "I see Jax every week and she stays with me when Emily's on tour. I miss them Jack, of course I do."

"So what's holding you back?" asked Jack. George was silent and looked down the cloisters as the early evening shadows stretched away.

Jack turned to face him. "Do you still love her?"

George stared at his brogues. He had tried so hard to put the memories of last year behind him. Now it felt like opening Pandora's box and sifting through feelings he really wanted to forget.

"It's not that simple is it?" he said. "It's never as simple as do you love her, yes or no. I struggle to find a form of words, despite the fact that I work in a library full of exquisite poetry describing every aspect of love. Besides, I can't talk about my feelings, I'm English!"

"Well try me," said Jack. "You explain and I'll try to understand."

George exhaled slowly and looked Jack in the eyes. "The best I can do is this. I thought we had a unique relationship - as close to perfect as we could be. I blessed every day we were together. Perhaps because she was often away, I valued the time we spent together even more. A year ago that changed overnight. There was a shadow over us and it's still there, all of those wonderful memories tainted."

Jack put his hand on George's shoulder. "Okay Georgie," he said. "Maybe you need some more time. Just remember this. Nobody's perfect. Perfection is for the birds. We're human beings, flawed and shaped by our imperfections and by our experience. You've placed Emily on a pedestal where no man or woman should be expected to stand."

They walked towards the door to the nave and Jack let them through. They looked upwards to the vaulted arches supported by the carved corbels and all the way to the quire.

"Exquisite, isn't it?" said George, his voice echoing in the silence.

"Yes it is. Exquisite. You know, maybe what you need is a little adventure."

George sat down at the end of a carved pew and traced his finger over the vine and grape carvings. He smiled up at Jack. "A little adventure? It's funny you should say that. Sit down and I'll tell you about my meeting with Jane Austen!"

Four

Whirligig Lane

George sat at the reception desk and looked down the long room to see where the noise was coming from. There was a ratcheting, squawking noise from the last window on the right, in the reference section. He walked slowly down the room, past the mahogany shelves which divided it neatly into bays on the left. Each bay had a pair of green leather and light beech side chairs, shaded wall lights and a low wooden table.

There were two students in the first bay, grinning and sharing a private joke on their screens. The next bay was empty, the third occupied by an elderly gentleman ensconced in the Times newspaper. George looked right and walked to the window. The sash was slightly open and there perched a rather defiant-looking magpie, its feathers gleaming blue-black with the morning rain, the long tail an iridescent green.

"Hello lovely," said George. "If you can't keep quiet, I may have to ask you to leave." The magpie looked at George and hopped a foot across the wide stone window ledge. "Fair enough, Squawk. May I call you Squawk? Just keep it down okay?"

The doorbell tinkled and George turned back to see a man of indeterminate age enter, look around nervously and walk to the reception desk. He had neat, short brown hair, parted at the side, was dressed in a long beige trench coat and held a cardboard box in front of him, like an offering in church. "Hello," said George, "may I help you?" The man put his box on the desk and coughed lightly:

"Hello, I'm Jim, I've come about the … you know, the books." He looked down at the half dozen volumes in the box and pushed them across the desk.

"Oh, thank you," said George, opening the first volume and recognizing the printed stamp of the original cathedral library. "Overdues by any chance?" Jim pushed back his chair as if he wanted to escape as soon as possible. He nodded. George ran the top volume, a plain grey-covered hardback copy of *The Tailor of Panama* across the scan pad in front of him.

"Right, yes, quite overdue," said George, looking at the screen. "About fifty years."

The man looked rather downcast. George felt sorry for him and gave his best sympathetic *long overdue* smile.

"Okay, Jim? Please don't worry, we're just grateful to you for returning the books after such a long time. Please come over to the table. Do you have a minute for a chat?"

Jim seemed reluctant to talk about the books and

waited until George ushered him to the other table. Then he took off his coat, looked around the room and sat down. "Lovely" he said, in a rolling midlands accent which reminded George of a Dudley comedian he enjoyed. "Never been here before. Lovely."

"Thank you," said George, taking a seat. "May I just ask you how the books came into your possession? Do you have any connection to the old cathedral library?"

"Oh no." Jim looked more comfortable and leaned back in his chair. "The books were loaned by Grandma. She worked at the solicitors here, you know, after the war."

"Cook and Greys, on the square?"

"Yes, that's right. Just round the corner. Worked there a long time. She loved her reading."

"And her name was?"

"Jill. Jill Munroe. Name should be on the ticket, well, computer now I suppose. How much is it then?"

"What?"

"The fine."

"The fine? Goodness, I think we'll overlook that. The cathedral library doesn't even exist anymore. We've been here since the eighteen-eighties and they passed all their stock on to us. This is a subscription library, run by a trust with the support of the university and the cathedral. Funds are rather limited at the moment Jim, so we're very pleased to receive donations. Or indeed, old books that find their way home to us!"

Jim straightened up and looked pleased. "Right," he said, "well that's okay then. Can anyone join? You know, the library." He waved his hand around the room.

"Yes, absolutely. I'll find you a leaflet. There is a modest monthly cost, with different levels of membership. Come back one day in the next week or so, my colleague Anne should be back by then and we can give you the grand tour."

There was a rustle from the stairs and Roxie swept by on her way out. She came over, looked at Jim, gave him a friendly smile and tapped George on the shoulder. "Sorry to interrupt," she said, "I left the history journals out for tomorrow, I hope that's okay? Have yourselves a good day." George grinned after her as she left, the tinkling bell and her jasmine-rose scent accompanying her exit.

"That's Roxie," said George, in answer to Jim's curious look. "Our resident historian."

"Lovely" said Jim, quietly.

"Aphra?" said Jules. "Call George please."

"Calling George," said Aphra. There was a click and then George's voice. "Good evening Jules!"

"Hey George, sorry, just wanted to catch you before Sense and Sensibility. Excited?"

"Absolutely. I've told Uncle Jack all about it. He's back for a couple of weeks, but I've hardly seen him. Always on a mission! You have your new virtual housekeeper then, Aphra?"

"Yeah, she's great, how did you know?"

"Bertie told me," said George, laughing.

"Bertie the butler? How's he settling in?"

"Very well, thank you, he's a cheerful fellow, good company too!"

"I'm glad to hear it. What did Uncle Jack think about the Jane Austen adventure?"

"Pretty much the same as you and I. Some kind of interactive role play, top quality, rather like a beta test. Not obvious who's created it and why we're involved. I think he'd like to join in, but I told him he's not one of the chosen ones!"

"Well, that sums it up I guess. I wonder what they have in store for us this time? Do you think we should do a stake-out, like in the movies. You in Beaton, me in Maine. Sunglasses on, hunched down in the car, half past eleven, watching the door."

"Jules, you've seen far too many stake-out movies!"

"Okay, save it up for another time maybe. I think we should consider finding out more about the Knightley Corporation and what they're up to. By the way, I think I'm more of an Elinor, but I am looking forward to meeting them both. I guess you know the novel was called Elinor and Marianne, before it became Sense and Sensibility?"

"You're right. Wasn't it listed as "by a lady" on the cover too? It still seems incredible that Jane Austen and the Brontë sisters had to publish anonymously at first. I made a sort of pilgrimage a few years ago to Winchester cathedral, where Jane Austen has three memorials. The brass one set in the floor praises *the sweetness of her temper,* but doesn't mention her writing. It seems like the Georgians were as prudish about reputations as the

Elizabethans!"

"Yeah, well I'm feeling like a time traveller to a distant land where women are second class citizens again. Okay, I'm off to the library, so I guess I'll see you in the nineteenth century."

"Bon voyage Jules!"

Five

Elinor and Marianne

"I wish, as well as everybody else, to be perfectly happy; but, like everybody else, it must be in my own way."

"Don't just stand there boy, take that tray in!"

George was adjusting to his surroundings, on the first floor of a sumptuous staircase in a Regency town house. A man on the ground floor in a plain black coat was shouting something.

"Pardon?" said George, looking down at the silver tray he was carrying.

"I said, take that tray in. Miss Dashwood and her guest are waiting for their tea!"

The penny sank. George realised that he was not a gentleman. He was a servant. "Oh, right, will do," he said.

"Yes, do!" said the man and hurried off down a corridor.

"Butler, by any chance?" muttered George and

addressed himself to the door in front of him. He looked himself over from the feet up. Black shoes, white stockings, mustard coloured breeches. Yuk! Dark blue uniform jacket with silver buttons. So, knock and wait. He knocked on the door in front of him.

Silence. George waited a minute, then knocked again.

Silence.

Gingerly, he reached out to the door handle with one hand, turned it and backed into the room with the tea tray. He set it down on a low table between the two armchairs. On his left was a lady he thought might be Miss Elinor Dashwood and to his right, could this be Miss Lucy Steele, conspicuous by her golden ringlets and attractive smile? He stood for a moment, looking from one to the other.

"Thank you Samuel, that will be all."

George had no idea what to do next. He walked slowly back through the door, closed it and stood feeling rather silly on the landing outside. He looked down the wide staircase to the ground floor where a gentleman in a green jacket, plain grey waistcoat and white cravat was waiting next to the hall table, his hat in his hand. There was no sign of the grumpy butler, so George moved down to the hall, his steps echoing on the polished stone chequerboard floor.

"Ah, good, there you are," said the man quietly. "Is Miss Dashwood at home?"

"Yes sir," said George.

"Mr Edward Ferrars," said the man.

Of course it was. He didn't look very much like

Hugh Grant, but then Miss Austen specifically noted that Edward was *not* handsome. Artistic licence! He remembered the scene in the book and wondered briefly if he should tell Mr Ferrars that his fiancée was also sitting in the drawing room upstairs, talking to Elinor, the love of his life. George decided to play his part, for now. He marched smartly back up the stairs, pursued by Edward, knocked, entered and announced, "Mr Edward Ferrars!"

The reaction of the two ladies was instant. They each tried to gather a smile, but only looked as though they wished they were anywhere else. Edward looked horrified as he saw both ladies together, Elinor Dashwood on one side, his fiancée Lucy Steele on the other. He took a moment to gather his wits, fixing an expression halfway between embarrassment and fear.

Elinor was the first to speak and welcomed Edward warmly and affectionately. She persuaded him to sit on the couch where he hovered on the edge of the seat. As she returned to her chair, George, still standing in the doorway was aware that she was looking at him enquiringly. He realised that he was expected to leave, so he bowed, not knowing what else to do and left the room.

George waited patiently in the hall. Where was Jules and what was the task this time? He looked at the gilt-edged oil paintings on the walls and then moved to the window where he looked out onto the street. He marvelled at the tranquillity of the scene, a boy leading a horse and cart, an open-topped barouche waiting outside the house next door whilst the driver leant on its door, smoking a pipe. He was interrupted by a maid who came running out of the corridor where the butler had disappeared earlier. She came up to him and grasped his hand.

"Please help me!" she said in a frightened voice.

George looked at her face. "My goodness, Jules!" Then he realised that she was laughing. "What was that all about?" he asked.

"It's lousy being a servant!" said Jules. "I feel like giving this up right now. I appeared in the kitchen, they made me clean the dishes and then the butler tried to kiss me in the pantry!"

George couldn't help himself and laughed out loud.

"It's not funny George! It's just as well we can only feel our hands, that's all I'm saying. I had to slap him in the face and he didn't say a word. I told him if he did it again I'd sue his ass!"

"You Americans, so litigious,"

"Well it's okay for you, what are you a footman or something?"

"Yes, I think so, do you like my buttons? I just served their tea in the drawing room. Elinor, Lucy and Edward Ferrars. They looked like startled pheasants, poor things."

"Okay, well I'm not going back in the kitchens, that's for sure. Great house, beautiful, just not below stairs right? Any sign of a task?"

A side door opened and the butler appeared, pacing slowly towards them.

"Oh no, not again!" Jules tried to hide behind George, still holding his hand. The butler walked up to

George and handed him an ivory card. He turned about and started ponderously back down the corridor.

"I say," George called after him. The butler turned around. "You should be ashamed of yourself. I might have to tell Mrs Jennings about your behaviour." The butler said nothing and continued through the door.

"Well that really told him," said Jules. "Is that how you defend a lady's honour? You could have punched him on the nose for me."

"Maybe later," said George. "Let's have a look at this."

The card said:

Please choose a task each:
Play the pianoforte with Marianne.
Borrow a book from the house library.

As they looked at the card, they heard the door open on the landing above and saw Elinor cross to the upper stairs. A few minutes later, Elinor and Marianne returned to the drawing room to join Lucy and Edward.

"Do you play?" asked George.

"Aye, a little, but very ill," said Jules with a mischievous grin.

"Well, alright then, *Miss Elizabeth,"* you win the piano and I will attempt to engage Elinor in a literary discussion. How many Georgian and Regency authors can you remember? They had barely invented the novel."

"It's going to be no picnic to talk to them on their own, George. They're not used to servants wanting to have a chat about Shakespeare."

"Well, they haven't met any servants like us, have they!"

George and Jules explored the grand hall, waiting for their opportunity to seek out Marianne and Elinor on their own. After a few minutes, Edward came out of the drawing room with a careworn face and hunched shoulders. Ignoring George and Jules, who were standing at the long windows, he opened the front door and was about to step into the street, when:

"Edward, wait!"

Lucy Steele ran down the stairs in a flurry of smiles, hat and parasol. She caught him at the door, put her arm through his and he ushered her out into the street. There was silence again until Marianne came quietly out of the drawing room and crossed the landing to the upper stairs.

"Right," said George, "you're on. Have fun!"

"You too. See you back here in ten." Jules moved up the stairs, past the drawing room, turned left and looked down the corridor to find the music room. She listened at the two doors she found. The first was locked; the second, on the right, opened revealing a large room with blue velvet chairs in two rows and next to the windows, a dark wood pianoforte. The long windows overlooked the street and beyond, a neat square garden with black railings and pleasingly straight ranks of horse chestnut trees. Jules spent a minute admiring the quality of the view and then turned her attention to the piano. "Okay then, let's see what happens when I make a racket."

She pulled out the piano stool and settled herself with her back to the windows and their deep crimson drapes. There were several pieces on the music rack. She recognised a traditional folk song called *Robin Adair*. Behind it were some Haydn sonatas and several hand-notated country dances.

Jules decided to start with something appropriate. She knew the chords for *Greensleeves*, so she placed her hands at *A minor* and started to play. The sound was unreasonably loud, especially in the relative quiet of the late morning. She decided to carry on regardless. Perhaps some singing would be in order. In her tuneful mezzo, she began:

Alas my love, you do me wrong
To cast me off discourteously
For I have loved you well and long
Delighting in your company,
Greensleeves was all my joy ...

She was interrupted by a knock at the door and Marianne entered, elegantly attired in an ivory dress over a lemon-yellow satin petticoat. She looked a little pale and tired but this did not detract from her beauty. Jules had stopped playing and stared at Marianne, who stared back. Marianne approached the piano with a gathering frown on her face. "What are you doing? You are the maid, Juliet, are you not? What are you doing in here … ?" She stopped as Jules stood up and smiled.

"My name is Juliet, I am a kitchen maid and I am playing the piano. Oh and I am very pleased to meet you, Miss Marianne." Jules held out her hand.

Marianne stared at Jules' outstretched hand and instead of taking it, placed her own on the back of the piano. "I don't understand," she said. "Are you unaware that servants are not permitted to play the piano? Have you no work to do? I should have thought that Mr Squires would have explained all this. Should I call him?" She moved towards the bell push, but the last thing Jules wanted was another encounter with the dreaded butler. "Stop!" she said. "Could you please listen to me for a moment and then I will leave. I promise."

Marianne sighed and sat on one of the velvet chairs. "Very well," she said. "I am tired, but you are new here so I will hear you for a moment."

"Thank you," said Jules. "I played the piano because it is a source of consolation to me. I understand from Mrs Jennings that it used to be a great comfort to you too, in times of disappointment. They said that you had not touched the piano since the troubles with …" she paused, "Mr Willoughby."

At the sound of his name Marianne looked out of the windows, as if this might spirit the memory away. "Are these your copies?" asked Jules, pointing at the sheet music, looking for a distraction.

"Oh, the printed ones come from Andrews, they are expensive so we make our own hand copies. Those jigs and country dances are mine." She smiled, seemingly glad to be diverted for a moment.

"I hope you will play again soon," said Jules, "it is good for the soul, or so they say."

"Music was my passion, until this year. Now I find that I cannot concentrate long enough to play a simple dance," said Marianne, tugging at her sleeves. "You were playing Greensleeves when I came in, where did you learn it? It is not a usual accomplishment for a maid."

Jules grinned. "I am recently arrived from the new world. Manners are very different there. It feels like I'm thousands of miles away now, in time as well as in space. It seemed quite normal for me to learn the piano when my family moved to Baltimore. We had no servants, I had to learn everything myself, housework, cooking, needlework and then the local school for reading and writing. Society is being re-forged there. Mr Jefferson, other political men and women, philosophers too, they all talk of equality for all. Imagine that! In any case, I will not be here in England for long."

"How so?" asked Marianne.

"I must return to the new world." Jules was silent for a moment and the only sound was the exquisite singing of birds from the square.

"Are those?"

"Nightingales, yes," said Marianne. "They are my favourite songbirds. They sing during the day here, many, many different songs, as if they are performing a new concerto each time."

"This is Berkeley Street, so that is Berkeley Square

then?"

"Yes, why do you ask?"

"Oh," said Jules, her hands returning to the piano. "I happen to know a song you may like. I can guarantee that you will not have heard it before. It's called, *A nightingale sang in Berkeley square.* It's an old standard where I come from." Marianne looked intrigued and sat up in her chair. "Please, I would like to hear it and then perhaps you should go."

Jules took a breath, remembering the last time she played the song. Then she began, slowly at first, finding the chords, softening her voice at the descending notes of the chorus. She started to sing the second verse but stopped when Marianne turned away. Jules could see that she was crying quietly into her handkerchief. She left the piano, moved to Marianne's chair and placed an arm gently around her shoulders. Back in the Maine library, sitting in the armchair, Jules felt her own eyes grow warm, tears starting to form and she wondered how they looked on the face of her avatar.

A bell sounded below in the hall and a shiver ran through Marianne. They both stood and she held out her hand. Jules took it and held it for a few seconds before she moved towards the door. "Goodbye Miss Marianne," said Jules, "Thank you for allowing me to play."

"Goodbye Miss Juliet. I believe that you are quite the most unusual maid that I ever met! Good luck."

Alone in the hall, George reflected on how he might engage Elinor in the library, as she was currently alone in the drawing room. Where *was* the library? He was about to climb the stairs when there was a knock at the front door. "It's busy here today!" He opened the door to reveal a young man holding out a small package. He was dressed in a scarlet jacket and grey waistcoat. "Are you a post boy by any chance?" asked George, grinning.

"Course I am!" said the young man, indicating his jacket. "That'll be one penny."

"Oh, money," said George, wondering if he had any. The post boy looked at him rather scornfully. "No money, no parcel."

"Right," said George, patting his waistcoat. He tried the pocket. There were two coins inside and he handed one to the boy.

"Thanks mate, very generous!" said the boy, thrusting the paper-covered package at George and running off down the street.

"You're welcome," shouted George, amused by the sight of him and the inventiveness of the virtual world.

Closing the door, he inspected the parcel with its brown paper and white string tie. There was no name, just the Berkeley Street address. He pulled the string and the parcel revealed a book and a card which said:

To Miss Elinor Dashwood. I saw this and thought of you. I look forward to discussing its merits. Sincerely, Brandon.

The book had a plain mauve card cover, no picture and

the title meandered across the whole of the front:

An historical and moral view of the origin and progress of the French revolution. By Mary Wollstonecraft.

George was unfamiliar with the work, but knew a little of Mary Wollstonecraft, one of the earliest advocates of educating women and promoting social equality. She held another fascination. She was the mother of Mary Shelley.

Time to seek out Elinor and the library! He strode quickly up the stairs, knocked on the drawing room door and found Elinor still sitting in her armchair, staring out of the windows to the manicured gardens at the back of the house. She looked up as he entered.

"Samuel?"

"A book for you, Miss. From Colonel Brandon." He handed her the book and card and stepped back. Elinor studied the book for a few seconds, smiled and placed it on the arm of the chair. "Any other messages Samuel?"

"No Miss. Just, um, a question Miss."

"Yes?"

"May I borrow a book from Mrs Jennings' library?"

Elinor turned and looked at him sharply, as if he had asked for a pay rise.

"Borrow? A book?"

"Yes Miss." George wondered if he would have to repeat everything twice.

"Do you read then Samuel?"

"Yes, Miss, I am quite a reader."

"Of what, may I ask?" Elinor's expression was a curious picture, somewhere between surprise and amusement.

"Mainly novels Miss. I particularly admire Mr Fielding and his *Tom Jones*."

"Well," Elinor seemed lost for words for a moment. "Mr Fielding is a rather notorious writer and is unlikely to be a feature of Mrs Jennings' library, extensive though it is." She thought for a moment and then stood. "Come with me, Samuel, let us take a walk."

Elinor led the way to the second floor and then straight ahead through double-leaf oak doors into the library. It was the most comfortable library George had ever seen; similar in size to the drawing room but furnished with leather armchairs, thick Persian rugs, ornate glass candle holders and objets d'art. Row upon row of mahogany shelving accommodated those smart bound volumes, typical of a gentleman's collection. George wished he could stay there for a week.

"Stay here," said Elinor. "I will return shortly."

George started pulling books at random from the shelves, to see if they were actual, fully-formed volumes. They were. He was amazed at the detail. Here were the diaries of Samuel Pepys, collections of sermons by Fordyce and Cooper, maps, memoirs, journals and biographies. In the far corner of the room George found a large bookcase of novels and on the top shelf, copies of Henry Fielding's *Tom Jones* and *Joseph Andrews*.

He turned at the sound of the door and in walked Elinor and Mrs Jennings. Fortunately, Mrs Jennings was smiling and he took this as a good sign.

"Well, young Samuel, only here a couple of days and already in the library eh? What shall we do with you? Quite out of the ordinary, would not you say Miss Dashwood?" Here, she gave Elinor a nudge.

"I do like to encourage the servants to learn their letters and read, Mrs Jennings," said Elinor. "However, I thought you would wish to approve any loan."

George moved to join them in front of the marble fireplace, a book in his hand.

"Oh yes, yes, quite right, but of course he must have a novel to read if he likes. We have all the poets and writers near here you know, it's quite the literary circle. That book Brandon gave you, I knew the name straight away. Mary Wollstonecraft! The poor lady, such a sad story and they lived just nearby. But her young daughter Mary! Such a dreamy little girl. Only last year, I saw her walking in the square, picking up the chestnuts, accompanied by two gentlemen who were close in conversation. "Miss Mary," I said, "good morning to you, would you do me the honour of introducing me to your father?"

""Oh Mrs Jennings" said she, such a bright smile, so *interested* in everything around her, "that is not my father, those are two of his friends, taking the morning air." And what did she do? She took me by the hand and walked me over to the gentlemen who were standing near the gates. They smiled indulgently at her as she approached, such good manners."

""Mrs Jennings, may I introduce you to my father's friends, Mr Wordsworth and Mr Coleridge." she said.

Well, can you imagine! We exchanged the usual pleasantries you know, but I could not wait to ask Mr Wordsworth about his poems. We walked and talked and he was like an old friend, telling me of his Lake District journeys. His friend was quiet and reserved. He seemed happy to look at the trees and point out the flowers to Miss Mary. Well ... "

"Forgive me for interrupting," said Elinor. "The question of the book? Which did you wish to read, Samuel?"

"I thought of *Joseph Andrews* Miss, but wondered if you might recommend something more ... elevating?"

"Quite so. Have you read Mr Richardson's *Clarissa*. You share his name, Samuel."

"No Miss. Not yet."

"Then you will find much to educate and amuse you. It is also very *long*."

"Thank you Miss." George turned to Mrs Jennings. "Miss Mary didn't mention anything about monsters did she ma'am?"

"Monsters? Good lord, whatever next! Monsters! The things you young people say these days." She looked at the glass clock on the mantelpiece and exclaimed "goodness the time, I am due at Mrs Palmer's. Good day." With that, she swept out of the room and the library fell into stillness.

George exchanged the reprehensible *Joseph Andrews* for the respectable *Clarissa* and walked back to the fireplace. He turned to Elinor. "Your meeting with Mr Ferrars and Miss Steele did not go well then?"

Elinor looked discomfited and confused by George's

familiarity. "No," she said and sat down in an armchair looking quite fatigued.

"I should go now," said George. "I truly admire your fortitude and patience. You are quite an inspiration."

"You are very free with your opinions, for one so young." said Elinor. "I usually consider myself to be modern, but I appear to have been left behind by these new ways. Then, perhaps it is for the best, after all."

"Yes," said George, deciding to ditch his character and try his luck. "You may find in the future that all people, not just those who are born as gentlemen and gentlewomen, are free to speak their opinions, to vote in elections and to go wherever their hard work and talent leads them. You would become accustomed in no time, I assure you."

Elinor looked at him as if he were speaking an alien language, which in a way, he was. George moved to the library doors. "Thank you for the book," he said, "I am sorry if I shocked you. I must go back to the future now, but first I have to punch your lecherous butler in the face. Good day to you."

Jules was waiting in the hall. "How did you do then Jules," he asked. "Mission accomplished?"

"Yes," said Jules, looking rather melancholy. "It was wonderful. And sad."

"Have you seen the butler, by the way? I have some unfinished business with him."

"No, but we must be close to the hour anyway. Did you manage to borrow the book? Oh, *really*?" Her face brightened at the sight of the book in his hand.

"*Clarissa*?" she laughed. "Good luck with that!"

They heard the door and saw the butler making his way towards them like a determined snail. He stopped a few feet away and said: "well done, you have achieved your appointed task. You may proceed to the next assignment." A green-edged door appeared next to the staircase.

"So are you going to apologise to the young lady for what you did, you odious man?" said George.

There was a brief pause. The butler straightened up, looked George in the eye and said slowly, "No."

George swung his right fist in the direction of the butler's head. He missed. Back in the library, he nearly fell out of his chair. Squires was quicker than him. George swung his left in an uppercut. Again, the butler swayed out of the way, like a lightweight boxer, showboating.

"Oh this is pointless!" shouted George. Squires stood still and silent. George looked at Jules who was giggling.

"Way to go, George," she said. "I think you'd better give it up."

George breathed out, dropped his hands and shrugged. "I agree, boxing was never my strong suit."

Jules turned her head to the left, distracted by a movement. "Uh-oh, time to go I think. I can hear someone at the door."

"Okay, I'll call you tomorrow," said George, moving towards the green exit. "That was intense and rather strange."

"Take it easy George." Jules put her hand on his

shoulder and they walked through the green edged door, the light fading from white to black.

Six

The stake-out

George opened his sitting room window and took in a long draught of the cool night air. The day had been unseasonably warm for September and families had been ambling around the cathedral fields until sunset, enjoying the mellow red and golden hues of autumn. A familiar-looking magpie landed on the edge of the balcony next door.

"Hello, is that you Squawk?" The magpie settled on the chrome bar, the green of its extra-long tail reflecting in the light orbs. "Hungry?" George threw some sunflower seeds on to the balcony. The magpie flicked its tail and flew down to the lawned gardens below. "Not much of a conversationalist are you?" muttered George and closed the window. He sat down at the dining table in the corner of the sitting room and opened a manila folder. Taking out a handwritten letter from the file, he set it on the table. His mind returned to the video-call from his friend Joe, just over a year ago, still fresh and sharp in his memory.

Joe had appeared on his sitting room wall screen, dressed in his usual Led Zeppelin t-shirt, his long fair hair loose around his face. "George, what's up buddy. It's been a while."

"Hey Joe, good to see you, all shipshape here, you know, Emily's away on tour and Jax is working hard at school. You?"

"Thanks man, just completing the links on these new solar arrays. It's pretty crazy here at the moment, they want this done by the end of the month and then the whole of Texas will be neutral. These new arrays can power the whole of Houston, no sweat. When the carbon filters come online next year, Texas could be the fastest state to be negative carbon. Amazing, eh?"

"Fabulous mate, you're sounding more American every time I see you. You'll be eating bagels in Greenwich village next. How's your friend Mia?"

"Oh, she's good." Joe paused for a moment, looking a little nervous. He smoothed his hair back from his face and sat up. "Actually, that's kinda what I wanted to talk to you about." He paused again and looked down, as if to check some notes. "Listen mate, I don't want you to take this as a hundred percent. It's … I guess you'd say a rumour. About Emily."

George felt his stomach tense and he pushed his fingers into his palms. "About Emily? What about her?" he asked.

Joe looked down again and then back at George. "So, it's really an odd co-incidence. Mia was in Frisco in May, staying with her mate Brigitte. They go way back, friends since high school. Brigitte is a make-up artist at the War Memorial Opera House. Anyways, she's telling Mia all about this touring production of Don Giovanni at the opera, and all about the lead guy, Anthony Russo." He paused again. "I'm sorry man, this is not easy to say. Well, Brigitte and the other make-up guys backstage were all having a gossip about these two women he was seeing. So … Emily's name came up. I asked her if she was sure of the name. I thought it couldn't be her. I even asked Mia to phone Brigitte to make sure they were talking about the same person. I didn't want to tell you but it's been eating away at me and I asked myself, would I want to know? I'm not sure, I guess I would. You're my oldest friend. I didn't know what to do or what to say." He paused again. "Look George it may be nothing, you know how people talk. Ask Emily, see what she says, it may be some stupid misunderstanding, I don't know … " He trailed off, looking deflated.

George looked away, took a deep breath and tried to muster a smile. "Joe, look, thank you for your honesty. As you said, it's a difficult judgement. I'll talk to Emily. I'll let you know what she says. It could just be malicious gossip, we don't know."

Joe looked relieved and smiled. "Okay man, keep me in the loop. We'll have a chat soon, yeah?"

"Absolutely. Take it easy Joe."

George came back to the present and realised that he had been staring at the blue swirls of the Robert Delaunay painting opposite the table for a full five minutes whilst the memory of the conversation played back like a film in his mind. The print, *Simultaneous Windows* had been a gift from Emily for his thirtieth birthday. He loved the way the light refracted from the deep blues to the gold, with the mysterious architectural figure at the centre. Trying to concentrate, he brought his disobedient attention back to the handwritten letter in front of him. It was dated two weeks after his conversation with Joe, when Emily had returned from the tour.

Summer view Terrace

Dear George

I'm so sorry I ran off like that. I wanted to explain it all to you but I couldn't think, couldn't even express myself clearly. I've come back to my mother's old house and I'm sitting here surrounded by dust sheets, pots of paint and a thousand memories. They're as fresh as the paint on the walls. I miss her so much George! And now this.

You wanted to know the details and you have a right to know the truth. If the roles were reversed, I would expect the same from you. We are rational creatures George, most of the time. Occasionally, we uncover a different nature.

We arrived in San Francisco on 15ᵗʰ May for two weeks of performances. I was singing in the chorus. This much you know. You may recall Anthony, you met him at the Welsh National Opera in Cardiff, do you remember? I think I told you, people believe him to be vain and egotistical, but really he is quite considerate and thoughtful behind his macho media image.

It was the weekend in San Francisco, half way through the Don Giovanni run, which was a sell-out. The whole company was excited. I called you from the Victorian Hotel, just after the Saturday evening performance, do you remember? We were all going out to the Blue Jays Bar for cocktails. Anthony tagged along (he didn't usually come out for drinks and preferred to protect his voice).

It was really the first time I had the opportunity to talk to him about his world outside opera. He spoke quietly and respectfully. He was also a very good listener. I knew about his reputation, of course, but I didn't see why that should affect me. We wouldn't be alone, after all. We sat on a corner sofa with Maurice, Lucy and Sandro under a rather tacky fake palm tree and I talked about my mother, for the first time in weeks. It felt as if the music and the laughter allowed me to step outside of my grief for an evening. To be myself, normal again, for a few hours. We stayed there until about one in the morning and walked back to the hotel. We all said goodnight in the foyer.

Anthony had a suite on the top floor and he asked if I would like to see the view. Writing this down, it feels like a ridiculous cliché. And like the worst kind of fool, I accepted. George, if I could only rewind and take a different turn!

We were both quite drunk. Anthony poured some

wine and we looked across the city and out towards the bridge. If I say it was like a fairy tale, you can see that I felt more as an actor in a play, than a real person. I was in a real sense "out of my mind". It wasn't just him. We ended up, as the Americans say, "making out." I'm embarrassed just writing it down. I'm not going to give any more details in a letter. I will tell you if you ask. We both fell asleep on the couch and I went back to my room in the morning. One of the assistant directors, Suzie was standing in the corridor waiting to speak to Anthony when I left his room. She must have told someone what she saw and other people made their own conclusions, as they always do. I'm so sorry George. I made a big mistake, I breached our trust. It will not happen again.

Anthony was polite and apologetic when we spoke before the next performance. He said he would speak to Suzie. As far as I was concerned, that was the end of it.

I have to ask you this. Haven't you ever done something that stupid?

I will come home when I've met Jax from school and I hope we can talk in the evening. Please believe me when I say to you that I love you as I have always loved you. With all of my heart.

Emily

George put the letter away in the folder. He rapped his

knuckles on the table and stood up. "Bertie, call Jules please."

The large sitting room screen switched from the slow-moving image of a mountain stream cascading into a Scottish loch, to their avatar pictures and a piano tone. A few seconds later, Jules' face appeared.

"Hey, if it isn't prize-fighter George, back from the nineteenth century!"

"Very funny Jules. How are your washing-up skills?"

"Mm, they need a bit of work. I might practice some more piano though, you never know when it might come in handy."

"Absolutely. Any issues with the security guard? And no chat with Miss Austen this time?"

"No problems here. We have quite a few staff working late and me sat in a chair in the corner of the library waving my arms around is pretty normal."

"So why do you think Miss Austen didn't appear? I was hoping to ask her a few more questions."

"No idea. I guess we have the basic information we need. I would like a copy of the terms and conditions though. See what we signed up for!"

"Agreed. Let's see if we can ask next time." George paused. "Jules, are you enjoying this? I mean, I'm thrilled by the whole experience, strange though it is. How about you?"

"Sure, having a great time. I'm not too bothered about the whole mysterious, anonymous Saturday evening thing. It's just a game isn't it?"

George thought for a moment. "Well, yes it's a

game certainly. But quite an expensive one. I still don't understand why they chose us. Why not just beta test it like every other piece of software?"

"No idea. I've seen experimental virtual reality before, but nothing at this level."

George grinned. "I think it might be time to try your stake-out idea. What do you think?"

Jules laughed. "Go for it George! I had a good look around the reference section where I was told to sit and there's nothing out of the ordinary. This new tech though, I expect it's tiny. They can project a hologram from almost anywhere. The glasses and gloves stay under the chair, so nobody needs to come in for that. I guess it's pretty low maintenance. I wish I had a midnight rendezvous like you, it's not the same at seven o'clock!"

George smiled. "It's a little spooky, especially in an old building where the oak beams creak in the night. I think I'll just see who comes in the half hour before midnight. We have recordings of the front desk and there's nothing spectacular there, I've checked. Some of our gold key holders keep pretty strange hours but the touch pad keeps logs. I thought I might stake out the back entrance, see if we have any interlopers. I meant to ask, is Patrick okay with you staying late on Saturdays? How about your colleagues?"

"It's no problem George, Patrick's always happy to kick back and watch old movies and eat pizza with the kids. They watched the whole *Back to the Future* trilogy in one weekend. Loved it! I can't get enough of this new building, still working out where everyone is.

We have parks and recreation next door, they're a bundle of laughs, but I wouldn't stay too long, they might lure you over to the dark side."

"Right, I'll just don my stake-out suit and arrange an appropriate car for Saturday. What do think, a '58 Chevy or a Tesla?"

"The Tesla would be warmer and you can take Bertie with you."

"Good point, you're full of bright ideas."

"That's what I'm here for! Catch you later."

"Bertie, could you order me up a Tesla for Saturday night please?"

"Yes sir. What time?"

"I'll have it for six pm I think, until noon Sunday. I'd like to take Jax out for a little tour."

"Very good sir. Would you like it pre-warmed?"

"You spoil me Bertie. Will you be able to link to the car's cameras?"

"Yes sir. Would you like wine and canapes in the car?"

"Bertie, what the …?"

"I'll take that as a no then sir."

It was late on Saturday evening, the floodlit cathedral casting long night shadows, the greens misty-cool. The shiny red Tesla pulled up outside the apartment block and powered down, its quiet electronic tune reduced to a whisper and then silence. As George approached the driver's door, the handle popped out.

"Welcome Mr Sanders," said a chirpy female voice. "Would you like to drive?"

"Er ... no thanks," said George. "Carry on. Whirligig Lane car park please."

"Whirligig Lane, five minutes." The car pulled quietly into the road and hummed towards the library. "I will never get used to this," muttered George as he watched the steering wheel turn on its own and the car move smoothly down the road.

"She sounds nice," said Bertie.

"Oh, you're here already, welcome on board," said George. "I'd like to make a half hour surveillance video of the rear of the library, covering the back entrance and the fire escape."

"Yes, sir. The video may be low quality."

"Why?"

"It's dark, sir."

"Right. Well, we'll just have to make do, won't we."

The car pulled in to the parking zone and the street lights awakened to illuminate the tree-lined space. George took the wheel and moved the car a little further from the rear entrance, parked side on to the building and settled down to watch. He had rarely looked at the old building from this side and he trained his gaze across the three stories of geometric Georgian windows and then up to the smooth slate roof which housed the attic rooms. In the glow of the lights, he noticed a flutter of wings high up on the eaves. Swallows? No, these were smaller and flightier, skitting in odd directions. Bats perhaps? Bats in the belfry! Well, that would be appropriate for a library. Very Edgar Allen.

For the next ten minutes, nothing stirred. George decided to take a walk around, so he made a brief tour of the building and then came back to the car. He was considering catching up on the news, when he saw a light come on outside the back entrance. A slight figure emerged, hooded and cloaked, with a light female step and walked slowly away from the building to George's left, back towards the main road. As she walked, she looked twice across to the car.

George lowered the window to see better, but even with the street lamps, it was difficult to see beyond the cloak. "Did we catch that Bertie?"

"Yes, sir, I'll link it to your phone."

George closed the window and was just making himself comfortable again when there was a loud knock which made him jump like a spooked cat.

"Bloody hell!" he exclaimed.

A face appeared, the hood now pulled back, revealing a bush of dark hair, thick round glasses and vivid pink lips.

"Goodness, is that you Poppy?"

George lowered the window to reveal Poppy Pring, smiling broadly and with more than a hint of mischief in her wide eyes. "Hello George, I saw you from the upstairs window, skulking round the car park. Why didn't you come in, you do work here after all?"

"I, ah ... was checking the security, that's all Poppy. I am going in actually, a little late video conference with our colleagues across the Atlantic." He paused. "So, what brings you to the library this evening Poppy? I didn't know you were a key holder. Just a minute, I'll hop out." George jumped out of the car as Poppy stood back.

"I don't have a key myself," she said. "The Professor lets me in and I come out the back door. It closes itself," she added, looking towards the entrance. She had a curiously blithe way of speaking, as if she cared little for what she was saying and might just as easily be reciting a poem to amuse herself.

George didn't want to start a discussion about the whys and wherefores of access at this time of night, or indeed about what Poppy and the Prof were doing together. He made a mental note to remind all users of the rules and to have a word with the Professor about security.

"Right, okay Poppy, do you mind me asking which facilities you use after hours? Just out of interest, as it were."

"Oh," she laughed, "the Prof has introduced me to hologram chess, on the second floor. It's very exciting, I'm sure you've played haven't you George?"

"Yes, absolutely, it's great. I didn't know the Prof was a game player."

"Oh, he's surprisingly fun underneath that gruff exterior." Poppy looked around and shrugged. "I'd better be off," she said, raising her hood over her hair. "It's getting misty. And late."

"Yes, of course. Well, goodnight." George stepped back into the car and watched Poppy as she walked away, unhurriedly. He picked up his phone from the centre console.

"Bertie, does Poppy Pring, resident of Beaton, have any social media?"

"Just a moment sir, searching. Right, here we are. She is a member of the First Folio book club and a Scottish country dancing society. Her mother appeared in a local article on the benefits of outdoor pilates for seniors in independent living homes. Her dating profile lists her interests as reading, rambling, chess, comic book conventions and dungeons and dragons."

"Wow, okay." George sat back for a minute, looking up at the eaves to see if the little creatures were back.

"Bertie, did Uncle Jack change your settings?"

"Yes, sir."

"To what?"

"Full personality sir."

"And what is that?"

"The full personality mode uses the accumulated experience of the home manager to create a friendly and helpful house companion for the user."

"Well thanks, I wish I hadn't asked. Is it appropriate to ask if you like this mode?"

"Oh yes sir, Uncle Jack said my accent was pucker and I had the gift of the gab."

George laughed. "He's not wrong there."

Seven

Mansfield Park

"There are as many forms of love as there are moments in time."

George settled into the armchair on the second floor waiting for the cathedral bell and he hoped, the appearance of Miss Austen. He had received a card invitation which was left casually on his keyboard on Friday. It said simply, *Saturday, Mansfield Park*.

At precisely midnight, the bells started to sound and the familiar figure of Miss Austen grew into life next to the book shelves. "Good evening George."

"Good evening Miss Austen."

"Are you familiar with Mansfield Park, George?"

"Yes. I did some homework yesterday though, a little refresher."

"What is your opinion of the novel, say in comparison with my other works?"

"Well, far be it for me to rate a novel in front of the

author, but I would venture to say that for many readers, it's their least favourite. Not for me though. In fact, I find it just as rewarding as Persuasion."

"Do you indeed? Many readers find Fanny Price simply too good, too correct, perhaps too perfect."

"That is true," agreed George, "especially for the modern audience. It's the Cinderella syndrome, perhaps she's too wholesome to be completely likeable. But I think the other characters come alive in contrast to her. The ghastly Mrs Norris, for example. Could she be the nastiest character in your books? Her name was even used for a nosey, interfering cat in the stories of a certain boy wizard."

Miss Austen paused and smiled. "You are correct. Do you have any other thoughts before we begin?"

"Well, the ending is very much of its time and perhaps more comfortable for nineteenth century readers than for us. The Crawfords are to my mind beautifully drawn, complicated, selfish in a contemporary way, scheming and manipulative. They leap off the page!" He waited for a second. "There is one query. Jules and I would like a copy of the terms and conditions of these little excursions. Is that acceptable to you?"

"Certainly," said Miss Austen. "You will receive them shortly."

In the Maine library, Jules took a sip of beer from the bottle at her elbow, settled down in her black swivel chair and placed the glasses over her eyes. The Jane Austen figure had vanished after a brief exchange of views on the acceptability of *Mansfield Park* to American readers. Jules was not a devotee of this, the most *challenging* Austen novel.

She raised her gloved hand and pointed forwards. The white screen dissolved and a gravelled courtyard materialised in front of her, leading to a meadow and an avenue of horse chestnut trees marching majestically into the distance. She could see stables to her right and turning left, a gravel drive which swept round to a large red brick house with grand white columns guarding the front door. Turning fully around, she saw a brick archway which lead to a side entrance and rose garden. She could feel the light autumn breeze on her hands and glancing down, plain black shoes and pants! What was this? She examined her clothes as far as she could, black waistcoat, a fob watch in the pocket … then she was startled by a running step on the gravel and the appearance of a panting footman out of the archway from the rose garden.

"Mr Baddeley, Sir Thomas is asking for you. Sorry Mr Baddeley."

"Thank you," said Jules and followed the footman to the side of the house and round to the kitchen garden entrance. "You have to be kidding," she muttered as she hurried to the back door, "it looks like I'm the butler!"

The footman led the way down a tiled and whitewashed corridor. Jules hurried to keep up as they passed the kitchen, clouds of steam billowing out of the door, a storeroom full of red and gold feathered pheasants on a rack and an office with a painted sign saying *Housekeeper*. Passing the office, the footman opened the large black door at the end of the corridor and they came to a vestibule which led to the main hall. "Sir Thomas was in the morning room, Mr Baddeley," said the footman, then lowering his voice, "there may be a problem with the wine." He turned quickly back to the kitchens, leaving Jules peering nervously towards the hall.

"Ah, Baddeley, there you are." A tall, grey-haired man in evening dress came across from the foot of the stairs. Jules was drawn to his ice-blue eyes and kind expression. "Sir Thomas?"

"I was expecting you in the ballroom, Baddeley, is there a problem?"

"No Sir Thomas, I was just … signing for supplies. They were late."

"Well, not to worry, we will need you in the ballroom shortly, the dancing is about to begin. We have many thirsty guests. Could you check the drinks please Baddeley, I saw the claret and cordial waters, but no madeira. You know how popular it is these days?"

"Yes sir, I'll see to it." An idea was forming in Jules' mind, that George may be in a similar situation. There was no sign of him. She doubled back to the kitchen corridor and knocked on the door marked *Housekeeper*. "Come." said a voice. Jules opened the door to reveal a small room with a simple desk and chair by the window, a dresser with picture plates and two women drinking tea at a low table; one evidently a maid, the other dressed in a long, plain, dark dress. Jules smiled and said, "I don't suppose either of you have seen George? The librarian?" The maid looked confused, but the housekeeper laughed. "Please come in Mr Baddeley. Thank you Rose, that will be all for now."

The maid left and Jules started giggling, the housekeeper joined in, laughing gently and then letting out great high pitched hoots, her body shaking with mirth and strands of her auburn hair coming loose from its bun. Jules plumped down in the armchair.

"How do like my pants?" she said, still giggling.

"Super. How do you like my dress? I had a bit of a shock when I arrived and looked in the mirror! But I rather like the idea of being a housekeeper. Where were you?"

"In the garden. Then Sir Thomas asked for some madeira for the guests. So this is the ball scene? Fanny dances with Henry Crawford, the ball is in her honour."

"Quite right," said George. "By the way, you have a man's voice and I have a woman's. We had our own voices in the other two novels.

"So we do. That's funny. Anyway, do you have a task?"

"No, do you? You're the butler! I thought the maid would have it but she just came in to ask about cheese. What do I know about cheese?"

Jules patted her waistcoat pockets and pulled out the watch chain, a small pipe and a card. "All right, here we go. It says:

Mr Baddeley and Mrs Bilberry, oh that's charming, it suits you George. *It is your task to ensure the smooth*

*running of the ball. If you have any questions, please
ask Mrs Norris.* That's it."

George stood up. "Mrs Norris? Old scary drawers? This should be interesting. We'd better make a start!"

"Better had." They stood looking at each other for a moment before Jules led them out into the corridor. George stopped a footman who was carrying a drinks tray and asked him to arrange for madeira and more glasses to be sent up to the ballroom. They walked through to the hall and watched as two handsome couples promenaded around, seemingly glad to enjoy the chance to view the house of Sir Thomas Bertram.

"Jules, you shall go to the ball!" said George.

"Well thanks my fairy housekeeper, that'll be the first since my school prom. I'm not exactly dressed for dancing though. Where's the ballroom?"

"I've no idea." said George.

They waited for a few moments until two footmen with empty silver trays came down the stairs. Following the sound of conversation and the tentative notes from a small group of musicians warming up, they moved slowly up to the first floor, along a wood panelled corridor and finally into the ballroom, brightly lit by hundreds of candles, in lamps, on sconces, in candelabras on every sideboard. The effect was transfixing. "My goodness," said Jules, "that's wonderful!" They moved to the side of the room and were watching two violinists playing a pretty duet when a loud voice carried over the music.

"Mrs Bilberry, Mrs Bilberry, where have you been?" A middle-aged lady in a purple ball gown, scowling under her stiff golden curls hurried over to them. "The windows, Mrs Bilberry, the windows!"

"Yes," said George, "what about them?"

"We agreed to have six windows open. There are only two. The dancers will need a breeze, will they not?"

"I'm sure they will, leave it to me." George shrugged his shoulders and moved along to the sash windows. As he pulled down the upper sash, he heard a crash. Turning, he saw a footman trying to retrieve a bottle and broken glasses from the floor, hindered by the lady in purple who was buzzing around like a fly, pointing and sighing. "Mr Baddeley, can you help? The couples will begin any minute and this will not do!"

Jules had been watching with amusement and now walked over to investigate, whispering, "Mrs Norris, I presume?" to George. Before she could assist, Sir Thomas strode into the ballroom, smiled graciously at several friends and then came to their side. "Mrs Norris?" he said, "would you please assist Lady Bertram with the layout of the card tables in the Orange Room?"

"Of course, Sir Thomas, but I cannot be everywhere at once! I … "

"Enough, Mrs Norris, please come with me, I am sure that Mrs Bilberry can manage here." He wound his way across the ballroom to the orchestra and then back to speak to a young lady seated quietly on a sofa nearby. The violins had stopped and the musicians were evidently waiting for the couples to form up for the first dance.

"Oh that must be Fanny Price!" said Jules, leaning

towards George. "The cross and necklaces, she looks so beautiful." Fanny was wearing a shining white dress, a present from her uncle, a very pretty amber cross on a simple gold chain and a second, longer, more decorative gold necklace. Her soft dark eyes shone in the candlelight. The effect was simple and elegant.

"They have her perfectly," said George. "William's cross, Edmund's gold chain and the Crawfords' necklace. This ball is like a microcosm of the whole novel in one bright evening." He clapped his hands. "Marvellous!"

The happily chatting couples congregated in the Orange Room and then formed a procession into the ballroom, led by Fanny and Henry Crawford, with Edmund and Mary Crawford second in line and the other half dozen couples following. They walked gracefully down the room until they reached the orchestra which, after a nod from Sir Thomas, began with a scotch reel.

George and Jules would have been perfectly happy to spend the next half an hour admiring the candlelit dancers, their figures and steps, but they were only allowed a few minutes before -

"Mrs Bilberry? I am sorry to disturb you." The maid, Rose, had crept quietly up to George. "One of the ladies is in a pickle, she's torn her dress. She's in the hall with her chaperone, a bit tearful."

"Well, that won't do, will it?" smiled George, "we can't have tearful ladies at a ball. Come with me." He led her back down to the hall where a very young lady in a turquoise gown was sat on a side chair whilst her chaperone looked on with a concerned expression.

"It was that clumsy oaf Charles, he stood on my dress, look!" she blew her nose into a handkerchief and spread the hem of her dress to reveal a foot-long tear."

"Oh my dear," said George, strangely enjoying his part, "that *is* a shame. Courage Miss, I'm sure we can help. Rose, do you know where Mrs Chapman is?"

"Yes Mrs Bilberry, she's helping in the kitchen."

"Please ask her to come here and see if she can pin this up so that Miss …?" he looked at the young lady, whose face appeared altogether brighter.

"Maddox."

"Thank you. So that Miss Maddox may return to the ball.

"Yes Mrs Bilberry."

George ushered the little group towards the vestibule and headed back up to the sound of lively jigs and merriment. At the ballroom entrance he was greeted by an unwelcome sight; Jules was leading a russet-haired gentleman and holding a bloodied handkerchief to his nose. The pair were pursued by Mrs Norris who was complaining loudly about rucked carpets and clumsy gentlemen.

"Hey George," said Jules with a sigh. "They're leading us a merry dance, that's for sure."

"Allow me," said George, "let's take him to the kitchens. Ice!" he shouted, "we need ice!" and he took the gentleman by the hand and led him down the stairs. Turning, he added, "Mrs Norris, would you, could you, accompany us please?"

For the first time that evening Mrs Norris looked

pleased to be involved. She followed them down to the kitchens where George set Colonel Harrison, for that was his name, in an easy chair with an ice pack for his nose and a glass of brandy for his nerves. Mrs Norris stood next to him and described the beneficial effects of sitting down.

George waited until a sense of calm was restored and then addressed Mrs Norris. "Might I have a brief word in my room? Thank you." He showed her in and stood with his back to the door, placing his hands behind him. Reaching out, he felt for a key in the lock and was pleased to find one.

"Mrs Norris," he said, "your assistance is no longer required. Put your feet up and enjoy the rest of the evening!" He turned quickly, opened the door, stepped out, closed it, locked it with the key which he slipped into his dress pocket, grinned and walked back to the hall where Jules was waiting.

"So where's Mrs Norris now, she's really grinding my gears!" said Jules.

"Oh," said George, cheerfully. "I think she's enjoying the undeniable benefits of a good sit down. I locked her in."

"Awesome! I really want to see Edmund and Mary Crawford close up. You want to join me?"

"Absolutely, lead on."

Back in the ballroom, the dancers were enjoying a quadrille, their figures describing elegant shapes in the candlelight. Jules and George circled the dance floor until they drew close to a petite lady with short dark hair in earnest conversation with a gentleman on a sofa.

Jules was struck by the lady's sparkling dark eyes and the gentleman's unhappy countenance. He was clearly troubled by the conversation. "I think that's Mary Crawford and Edmund," said Jules, pausing near the sofa, "I don't like to eavesdrop, but I can't resist."

Mary was clearly trying to be lively and coquettish. "Oh my *dear* Edmund, I do so wish you would choose another profession. The very *idea* of your standing in draughty pulpits week after week, meeting dull people and talking of dull provincial marriages."

"Miss Crawford," said Edmund, unimpressed by her humour and attempts at levity, "your objection to my choosing the clergy is surely not a result of conviction, only of the desire to provoke and vex me."

"But Mr Bertram, I do take you seriously. That is why I protest, in whichever manner I may try, and wish to find you a new profession."

"Thank you Miss Crawford, for your efforts, but my mind is quite made up. You will not dissuade me. Let us not discuss this now, this ball is in Fanny's honour and we should try to be happy for her." Edmund stood, bowed to Mary Crawford and left the ballroom.

As they listened, George and Jules watched a glowing Fanny Price dance past with her brother William, the pair in high spirits. Jules turned to speak and as she did, she noticed the light dimming behind the musicians, the effect starting to spread down the room, as if the candles were disappearing one by one. "George, what's happening?" she asked.

"I was going to ask you the same thing."

Suddenly, the music stopped. The dancers froze, as

if they had become part of a three-dimensional painting, their expressions fixed in time. George and Jules did not move, they only stared. "What do we do?" whispered Jules.

"Wait, I suppose. I think the programme is either broken or paused."

George walked over to the nearest dancer, a young lady in a bright green ball gown. He reached out and touched her hand. It was like a waxwork. "This is very strange," he said. "Rather like that odd fantasy people have where the world stops and you can go wherever you like until it starts again." A moment later, they heard a cough behind them and Jules screamed. Turning, she saw a man in grey evening dress standing next to a green door outline, with the word *Exit* above it.

"Goodness, you frightened me!"

"Please accept our apologies madam and sir," said the man. "You may leave by the green door. This adventure is finished."

Eight

One Year Earlier

"We can't carry on like this," said Emily.

George turned away from the window and his contemplation of the cathedral fields.

"Sorry, I was miles away. What do you mean, we can't carry on, of course we can."

"I mean, we can't carry on without communicating." Emily put down the music score she was reading at the dining table and walked over to George. She placed her hands on his shoulders and looked him in the eyes. "I know you're in there George, you've just built a wall around yourself. Nobody is allowed in, is that right?"

George sighed and turned back to the window. "Thanks for your thoughts Doctor Freud."

Emily reached out and turned him around. "We're having this conversation now, whether you like it or not. Since I came back from the tour you've been distracted, unhappy, maybe even depressed, I don't know. It's obvious that you're thinking about what happened on the tour and that's not surprising, of course it isn't. But you can't let this dominate your thinking for months on end. You have to create some new memories. You need to move on from this and so do I. It's in the past, like everything we've ever done." She kissed him gently on the cheek and laid her head on his shoulder. George reached his hand up to her short blond hair and stroked it for a second.

"I can't," he said and took his hand away. "I don't know why. I have every reason to forgive, to try to forget and to move on. It's reasonable, it's fair, but every morning when I wake up, the green-eyed monster is sat on the end of the bed, taunting me."

"Oh George! I appreciate the Othello metaphor but I hope you're not going to go crazy in a fit of jealous rage?"

"No, of course not."

"Please tell me what you need. If not for me, then for Jax, your friends and family."

"I'll try."

"I know it's difficult, especially when we have such a passion for our work. I could no more be a librarian than you could be an opera singer. But we're more similar than you think. You love your work, it's a part of who you are and I love that. It's the same for me. But I'm not an endangered butterfly, I'm not an angel. I'm just Emily. Look, straight fair hair, long Roman nose, freckles, just Emily." She paused, took a step back and sighed. "Listen George, you're not the only one who's felt that … sting of jealousy. You remember when we met?"

"Of course."

"You were still living with Virginia when you and I went out for dinner at the Boat House. You remember the bitterness when you left her and when she met me for the first time. It was awful."

"I do remember, I don't see that it's somehow similar."

Emily sat down in the armchair. "I'm not trying to suggest that. I'm asking you to think about the strength of *your* feelings and to consider that we've both acted in ways that have caused jealousy and resentment in those we love most."

There was a silence for a minute before Emily spoke again. "I've been thinking, we haven't sold Mum's old house yet. Maybe you need a little time and space for yourself. I could live over there for a month or so, see if that helps."

"You want to move out?"

"I don't want to, but as I said, we can't carry on like this. Look, I'll give it some more thought and we can discuss it tomorrow. Okay?"

"Okay."

"Please talk to your friends George. They're good for you. Talk to Joe and Ben. Have you spoken to Jules recently, she's great, full of good advice."

"Sure."

"I have to go to the recital, you haven't forgotten? You're collecting Jax from ballet.

"Yes, of course, go, you don't want to be late."

"I love you George."

"Yes, me too."

George was just about to take the first bite from his cheese and apple chutney sandwich when his phone rang. It was Jules.

"Are you okay? I got your message. Emily and Jax moved out? What happened?"

George looked longingly at the sandwich, stood up and closed the office door. This was his little sanctuary room behind the second floor counter, books piled high waiting to be catalogued, two threadbare grey armchairs and an old wooden tray with a green teapot. He was enjoying a late lunch whilst Anne looked after the enquiries desk.

"Hello Jules, thank you I'm fine." He sat back down and put his feet up on a large box labelled *Donations*. "We had a discussion at the weekend. Emily thinks I'm a poor dejected fellow and need a change. So she's moved into her mother's old house which we're selling. Or at least we were selling it."

"I'm sorry George, that's awful. Did she say for how long?"

"No, I think a month or so."

"You're going to see each other and Jax, right?"

"Yes, I'll see Jax every week. Emily and I will catch up when we can."

"Okay, well you kinda knocked me sideways for a minute there George. I thought I'd give you a call to see how you're doing."

"I appreciate it Jules."

"I'll catch you later for a proper chat okay?"

"Thanks Jules."

He put the phone down and reached for his sandwich.

He heard the lift doors close and there was a knock on the door. A cheeky face under blue-striped hair and a splash-patterned Dr Marten boot peered around the door. "Sorry to interrupt, George," said Anne in her sing-song voice, "the students have arrived early for their library tour. Shall I ask Handsome Raj to take it?"

George smiled. "Yes, thanks Anne, that would be great. If you could ask Raj to show them the holo-chess first, they'll enjoy that. I'll be along in ten minutes."

"Righto, enjoy your sandwich. Oh, by the way, Emily came in and left you a little present. It's on your desk."

"Thanks Anne, you're a treasure."

George joined the group of a dozen eager undergraduates on the first floor, where Handsome Raj was demonstrating the hologram chess. No one knew where Raj's nickname came from, but as George watched him talking enthusiastically to the students, he couldn't help thinking that it was rather appropriate. Raj himself was modest and unassuming, tall, always immaculately groomed and turned out in pressed chinos and button-down Oxford shirts. He seemed to like the way Anne said his name in her lilting Welsh accent.

The students took places on the black and white chequerboard whilst Raj and Anne directed the play. Each chess piece was a life-sized hologram character or a student player. Teams could choose from a variety of fantasy or historical themes. Today Raj had chosen medieval knights, the rooks flying their red or green battle flags from their turrets and each student wearing a holographic tabard with their team's colours. The chess pieces groaned and sighed when they were taken, the knights shouting "tally-ho!" as they zig-zagged across the board. "It's just like wizard's chess," whispered a girl on the red team. George smiled. It was good to see the students having some fun before the serious business of academic research started.

After a twenty minute game resulting in a swift and noisy victory for the reds, George showed the group the 3-D printers and led a short session on the advantages and equal perils of using voice-controlled assistants for research. "There are no short-cuts I'm afraid," he concluded. "You must quote every source and check its provenance. Thank you for coming, I'll see you all downstairs in five minutes. Please choose a book to take home, fiction or non-fiction. Reading, my friends, will improve your writing. I can show you research to prove it! You might enjoy it too."

George joined Raj at the computer tables. "Thanks Raj, they were a lively bunch. I'm glad they all joined in."

"Yeah, it's funny how much they like it here," said Raj, "I think it's more personal than the university building."

"Well we like to make everyone feel comfortable and at home, that's the secret." George patted Raj on the shoulder. "I don't know what we'll do without you at the end of term Raj. If you're free at the end of your placement, it would be great to have you back. Right, I have a group of technology students at three o'clock and you have an important meeting with tea and carrot cake, courtesy of Anne. Thanks again for your help."

"It's a pleasure George. I'll make sure they save some for you."

Back at his desk, George saw a small white box with the words *Guess the book, then you can eat the cake. E xx*, written on the top. Opening it, he saw a little butter-coloured sponge cake in the shape of a scalloped shell, sprinkled with icing sugar. A perfect madeleine. Letting his gaze rest on a postcard of Lombardy on the notice board, his mind wandered to the French summer countryside, the hazy heat of the afternoon, Marcel and his mother taking tea and cake under the garden parasol. He took a teaspoon and tasted the smallest bite, letting it melt in his mouth. Delicious.

He took out his phone, wrote, *Remembrances, Proust*, *yummy* and took another bite, reminding himself to save a little to dip in his tea.

After a short referencing session with the technology students, all of whom managed to stay awake, George helped Anne pass around small pieces of carrot cake to the students and other library users. "Do you think all libraries run on tea and cake?" said George.

"I do," said Anne, stacking the empty plates on a tray. "It's like the international language of librarians.

I used to help out at Aberystwyth public library where we had a cake and chat café to help people with their language skills. It was the best ice-breaker ever."

"I meant to ask, did you hear back from the literacy people about their new scheme?"

"I did, as a matter of fact, they're sending me the forms."

"Excellent," said George, "we could do with another string to our bow."

Nine

The Professor

"Please take a seat George." Professor Dobbs waved at a small side chair opposite the modern veneer desk. It looked somewhat out of place in the spacious first floor meeting room, with its cornices and large Georgian windows. He leant forward, picked up a slim typed report and showed the front to George.

"I imagine that you have read this?" said the Professor, his light, musical voice lending a contrast to his bristling eyebrows and intimidating expression.

"The Trustees' report? Yes, I received a copy this morning by email." George tried to sit up straight on the chair, but only succeeded in making himself more uncomfortable. He thought he knew what might be coming.

"The Trustees have asked me to brief you before they make the situation public. You have a right to know, as an employee. I should be grateful if you would

pass the information to your colleagues and the student librarians."

"Yes, of course."

"Well, as you have seen, it makes for uncomfortable reading. A financial loss in the last two years and reserves," he paused, as if looking for the correct word, "dwindling fast. We have bought little new stock in the last year and our subscriber numbers are flat. Did I leave anything out?"

"No." said George. He hadn't. That was a succinct summary of the woeful financial situation in which the subscription library found itself that September day. "But," said George, "we have engaged more local businesses for the small enterprise digital sessions and the 3-D printers are bringing in more money. We have also applied for some grants."

"Yes, yes, that is all to the good George. However, we have no choice but to look at ways of balancing the books. Or face … " He stopped and looked George in the eye. "Well, we needn't consider that at this precise moment." He stood up and started walking around the room, so that George had to rotate like a wooden top in his seat, to follow him.

The Professor continued, as if lecturing a group of students. "As well as exploring the commercial opportunities in the report, I thought we might consider something more … adventurous."

"Adventurous?" said George, his voice rising.

"A partnership. Beyond the University and the Cathedral."

"What sort of partnership?"

"I … that is, the trustees are considering some alternative uses for the building."

George stood up and faced the Professor, trying hard to hold his true feelings in check. "You cannot seriously consider … "

"Please, George sit down, these are simply ideas, suggestions." He waved his hand as if they were mere trifles. "The building is a significant asset, it would be foolish to ignore that, surely."

"The books and the staff are significant assets too," said George, wondering if there was any point in mentioning it.

"Indeed," said the Professor. "We've decided to allow another month to look at new funding. Selling the building may be the only viable option left on the table. The trustees would be grateful if you could all give it some serious thought. Let's leave no stone unturned."

George shrugged and stood up to leave. As he opened the door, he turned back. "Professor, there is one other issue we should give some consideration to. Security, that is access to the building."

"Security, what's the problem?"

"Well, as you know, all users are logged at the entrance during opening hours. Key holders have access from the back door. If they bring visitors, they should log them on the front desk scanner."

"Yes, of course."

"I bumped into Poppy Pring one evening. She … said that you let her in. It wasn't logged."

The Professor's eyebrows joined together to create a rather amusing caterpillar above his sharp grey eyes.

"Right yes, I remember. Of course, should have logged her in. My bad, eh George?"

"Yes."

"Well, an oversight, we'll all have to do better won't we?"

"Yes," said George, "we will."

George and Anne sat on the first floor sofas chewing over the Trustees' report. Anne stretched her hands above her head and exhaled slowly. "Some welcome," she said. "A couple of weeks holiday and I come back to this. George, do you really think they would sell the building?"

"I don't know Anne. It's hard to read the Professor sometimes, but I think he is serious about this. He believes it's the only option. We have to prove that it's not. We've always been able to rely on the university and fundraisers to make ends meet, but no amount of coffee mornings and author talks are going to fill this gap. We need some kind of Victorian benefactor like Miss Haversham!"

Anne, whose hair was now minty green to match her new boots, slapped the table. "I've got it!" she said, "we should sell books, not just lend them. What do you think?"

"Well it's a decent enough idea Anne, the only fly in the ointment is the Old Curiosity Bookshop on the square. They've been around for two centuries and I wouldn't want to try to compete with them! Or

Chambers on the high street, for that matter."

"Oh, that's true." She drummed her fingers on the coffee table, humming. "By the way, I gave a library tour to a chap called Jim who mentioned you. Do you remember him?"

"Oh yes, Jim. Quiet fellow, brummie accent, came in with some super-late books. Did he sign up?"

"Yes, he seemed pretty enthusiastic. After the tour, he sat down next to Roxie and I heard them chatting away like they'd known each other for years."

"Really, what were they talking about?"

"Bats."

"Bats?"

"Specifically Barbastelle bats. Apparently they're very rare. He said he'd seen them at night time flying around near the library. Roxie was fascinated."

George smiled. "Well, Roxie loves the little creatures. I've seen her feeding Squawk, you know, the magpie that perches on the windows? I saw something that could have been bats, around the eaves late one evening. They're very fast, not easy to see."

"If you say so George. Oh, look at the time! I'm due on the front desk." Anne scampered downstairs and passed Poppy Pring who was on her way up. Poppy looked like she was on a mission, headed straight over and slumped down on the couch next to George.

"Hello Poppy, everything okay?"

"No, George it isn't."

"Do tell, if you want to, of course."

Poppy took off her large glasses and started rubbing them vigorously on the hem of her skirt. "Professor

Dobbs is an idiot!" she said.

"Oh … what's he done?" asked George tentatively.

"Can't tell you. He's an arse. You know about the report?"

"Yes, we're looking at all the options. It's upsetting for everyone. I'm guessing this isn't just about the library though?"

Poppy stood up. "Is he in today?"

"Yes, I spoke to him earlier, in the meeting room."

"Right. I have to go, thanks George!" She grabbed her canvas bag and hurried over to the stairs.

"Okay, bye Poppy, good to see you … oh hello Kamal."

Kamal came down the stairs as Poppy went up. He had a pile of hardback books in his arms. "George, are you free?"

George opened his arms and gave a bemused smile. "Please, sit down Kamal, it seems that my consulting room is open for business."

"Oh, right." Kamal deposited the textbooks on the coffee table and sat on the sofa. He drummed his palms on his knees. "I think I've made a mistake, George. Quite a big one actually."

"Okay, well feel free to share. If you want to."

"Oh, I do," said Kamal. "I'm hoping you can dig me out of a hole."

"What sort of hole?"

"A … practical one really."

"Okay, start from the beginning and tell all, I'm intrigued."

"Right," said Kamal, "I shouldn't go too far back.

It's commercial, confidential."

George nodded. Kamal was a gifted postgraduate and George knew that several large software companies were courting his signature with large initial salary offers.

"So I asked my PhD supervisor if I could use the findings of my report, before it's published. She said that was fine, it was all quite vague, in fact she didn't seem very interested at all. I had some experimental graphene applications which I thought the automotive sector could use. Then a tech company emailed me and said they would pay me to use the applications and help me with the patent. I met them, they seemed legit, you know? I checked their credentials, they're based in the US."

"Go on," said George.

"I worked up the prototypes and we discussed them over video. They suggested some improvements. Then ... my supervisor calls me in and tells me that I've broken the rules and I may not be able to finish my Phd. I'm six months late with the submission as it is. They allowed the extension because the commercial application could be good for the university's reputation. But now they don't want the project to drift, they say the standard rules should apply to me, no exceptions, I need to finish it."

"Right," said George, feeling the need for more tea. "So what exactly are the conditions?"

"I have to give up any outside contracts and only work on my research until it's complete. No further extensions."

"Is that a problem? I mean, financially."

"Yes, it is. My funding has run out now. I need some income to complete the work, but they won't let me earn it. It's a catch-22 isn't it?"

"It certainly is Kamal. I would like a to have a think about it for a day or so? Maybe have a chat with your supervisor, off the record. Who is she?"

"Professor King. She's very helpful and fair usually. I have a couple of other ways to earn money, you know, the jazz band and some consultancy, but all that takes time too."

"Goodness, please don't give up the guitar playing, you're brilliant!"

"Thank you," said Kamal, looking embarrassed.

"Let's talk later in the week, is that okay?"

"Sure George, that would be great. Thanks."

Kamal walked over to the stairs and then stepped back to make way for Anne. She stood in front of George who looked up nervously. "Anne? Everything okay?"

"Tea's up." she said with a big smile.

George laughed. "Thank goodness for that!"

Ten

Northanger Abbey, Part One

"Friendship is certainly the finest balm for the pangs of disappointed love."

The mist curled around the base of the oak trees, winding its way along the path to a clearing, where it shone silver in the light of the half-moon. An owl hooted gently and the leaves whispered their story in the cool night breeze. Two figures appeared, materializing on the path near the clearing, their figures only half-visible, like a pair of wandering wood-sprites. The figures separated and looked each other up and down.

"You're a monk!" hissed Jules.

"So I am," said George, looking down at his brown robe. "And you're a nun, that's hilarious and rather … "

"George!"

"Why are you whispering?" said George, looking around the clearing.

"I don't know, it just seemed like the right thing to do. Oh great, this habit looks like an old sack." Jules pulled at the edges of her long black dress and grimaced.

"This isn't much better, to be fair. Funny, I don't remember any nuns or monks in Northanger Abbey, do you?"

"No, I don't. Really George, do I look as ridiculous as you do?"

"Oh … yes you do. Sorry." He looked again at Jules' habit and chuckled. "Right, I suppose we should have a good look around."

"Yeah, let's get out of this these woods, my hands are cold."

"Mm, it looks like springtime but my hands feel chilly too."

On the other side of the clearing, the misty path led through the trees and opened up to a meadow of long dewy grasses. As they emerged, Jules stopped and stared. At the top of the meadow there was a low wooden fence and beyond, the silhouette of a castle, its gothic windows glinting in the moonlight. To the left, the undulating silhouette of a ruined stone building, part of the old abbey. George joined her and they stood silently, watching. The cackle of a crow broke the spell and they moved irresistibly towards the castle.

Arriving at the fence, George noticed a card, tied to the post. "Excellent, no irritating butler to deliver the message this time, so what have we here." He read aloud:

Welcome to Northanger Abbey. Please enter the castle and find the Japanese box. Your task is within. Please do not awaken Miss Morland."

"Sounds like a piece of cake," said Jules. "I guess we just need to jump this fence and walk in the front door." She placed both hands on the top bar, pressed down and gracefully vaulted the fence.

"Impressive!" George stood back. "You look as if you've been practising. Right, here we go." George placed his left hand on the fence and launched himself over with his right. His avatar rolled the top bar and he landed on its back side on the ground like a bag of potatoes. "Whoops-a-daisy!"

"George, get up off your ass!" giggled Jules, "come on, let's see what's going on up there."

They made their way across the gravel to the front steps which led up to an arched stone doorway, with two pillars on each side and large, iron-clad double-doors. "What time do you think it is?" whispered Jules.

"I'd say past midnight, from the moon and the silence. I can't see any candles in the windows."

"Right." Jules tried pulling the huge iron door knob. It was firmly locked. "Round the back then?"

"I suppose so." George took a step back and looked around the castle frontage, taking in the walls of grey stone, the outline of the abbey cloisters on the left and the grove of ancient oaks watching over the meadows beyond. "Round to the right, I think. Servants entrance maybe?"

They explored the right hand wing and found a plain door which looked promising. This too was locked. Continuing around the castle, they came to an entrancing view. Here was an open terrace, lit with moonlight, leading to geometric shrubberies and water rills which spilled gently onto the lawns below. "George, over here!" Jules beckoned him over to one of the large sash windows. It was slightly ajar. She pushed it up with her hands and it creaked open.

"Now I feel like a cat burglar," she said, leaning in through the window. Once inside, they looked for a candle and found a pair of glass lamps with a spill on the mantelpiece, above the glowing remains of the fire. Touching the lit spill to the lamps, George watched as the room slowly filled with an orange glow which revealed row upon row of books, from floor to ceiling. Jules started to look at the spines of the books before George tapped her on the hand.

"One thing at a time Jules, we need to find the cabinet before we explore."

"Yeah, maybe later." Jules looked regretfully back at the shelves as they moved slowly out of the library. There were corridors running in all directions.

"Straight ahead, I think," said George, "wasn't Catherine's bedroom on the first floor?"

"Two doors down from Eleanor's." George shot her a surprised look.

"I read the book last week George, way of ahead of you."

"So it seems!" George raised his lamp and they made their way carefully to the main hall and up the stairs. The only sound was the ticking of a grandfather clock on the landing and the light click of their shoes, echoing in the silence. As they looked down the left wing of the house, they heard the creak of footsteps on floorboards. A sudden cold breeze blew along the corridor and extinguished their lamps. "Great!" said Jules, wondering how they would light them again. Their backs to the wall, they waited. A lock clicked. The door in the middle of the corridor groaned as it opened and a young lady's head, crowned with a white cap peered out.

"Who's there? Father? Is that you?"

They stood still and waited. The young lady looked both ways, ducked back into her room and shut the door firmly.

"Why didn't she see us?" said George, "it's not completely dark."

"I have an idea," said Jules. "Maybe we're ghosts, heard but not seen, relics of the ancient abbey." She waved her hands in mock ghostliness and George grinned.

They looked at each other and this time noticed that their gowns had an opaque quality, a light translucent glow.

"I think you're right, Jules. She didn't seem to see us at all. Our virtual masters seem to enjoy ringing the changes."

She smiled mischievously. "Should we start wailing, see if they can hear us?"

"Go ahead if you like. Only the clue said don't wake Catherine. I think we should carry on, at least we know where her room is."

They moved two doors past Eleanor's room and slowly opened the door to Catherine's. The curtains fluttered at the windows, strips of moonlight criss-crossing the floor. George walked past the four poster bed and there, as expected was the Japanese box. The box was in effect a large cabinet, black wood with yellow decoration, reflecting gold in the moonlight. There were two doors and a small key in the lock. George turned to look at the bed where Catherine Morland was fast asleep, the bed curtains half-drawn as if in protection from her wild imagination. Jules opened the curtains a little so that they could examine the cabinet. She tried the lock one way and then the other. It clicked and the doors finally folded back to reveal recessed drawers and a small door in the centre with a tiny key. She knew that in the novel, this little door revealed a manuscript which caused great excitement for Catherine. The tiny key finally yielded and Jules reached in for the manuscript. It wasn't there.

She stepped back and looked at George, opening her empty hands. He nodded and stepped in to investigate. Opening one drawer after another, George found nothing. Then he reached up and ran his hand along the top of the cabinet. His right hand touched a card which he pulled down for them to see. "I think this it is," he whispered, "we need to light the lamps."

They moved carefully out of the room and retraced their steps until finally they were back in the library with the lamps relit from the fire.

"Okay," said Jules, "read it out."

George took a closer look at the ivory card. "What in heaven's name is this?"

"Let's see." Jules moved closer and they read the card together. It said:

chef teacloth wolfsbane
Agnes Norry swimsuit
derisory hermits
demitri housefly photos

"Wow," said Jules.

"You know what this is?"

"I have no idea."

"Oh. Well, maybe it's a treasure hunt. We have to find the chef's teacloth and a swimsuit."

"And wolfsbane? Nice try George. It must be some kind of word play."

George looked again at the unlikely list of phrases. *chef teacloth wolfsbane*. What sort of clue was that? "Do you think it's a sort of cryptic crossword?"

"Could be. What we really need is a pen and paper." She looked around the room and crossed to the leather-covered desk which faced out to the gardens. "How about a parchment and quill?"

"Fabulous," said George. He joined her at the desk and they looked out across the manicured gardens. "So Jules, what are your thoughts on Catherine Morland?"

"Oh I like her! She has a strange feeling about the General, her imagination runs away with her, but she's right about him. He's a real jerk. In a Regency English way I mean."

"Mm, I agree. The book feels like Jane Austen's trying out this mock-gothic style. She doesn't use it again, but she does find a way for her characters to reveal themselves through their good principles or their prejudices. It's quite funny too!"

"Yes it is. I like Thorpe, he's hilarious."

There was a loud rap on the door. They froze. The door opened slowly and in walked a man carrying a candle. He was tall, with short grey hair and wore a light brown nightgown. "I heard voices, I know I did," he muttered as he crossed to the windows. He paused near the desk and stood staring at the two glass lamps. The breeze from the open window lifted the curtains and he walked within a foot of George, grabbed the lower sash and slammed it shut. George and Jules stood near to the shelves and watched. "Probably Henry," he said, reaching for the lamps and blowing them out. "Stupid boy, he'll burn the blasted castle down!" He took another look around the room and marched out, closing the door behind him.

"The charming General Tilney, I guess?" said Jules.

"Exactly. Charming. Right then, this clue, what's it all about?" They lit the lamps and looked again at the card. Jules took the quill, dipped the end in the ink pot and reached for a roll of parchment from the pile on the edge of the desk. She spread it out and several large drops of ink splodged onto the middle of the page. "Ha! Not as easy as it looks!" She tried again, this time tapping the quill on the edge of the ink pot. She wrote the letters from the first three words on to the parchment, but in a different order from which they were written. "How about an anagram?" she said.

"Brilliant!" said George. "Are you any good?"

"I have my moments." Jules looked again at the letters. "There's a *the* if it helps. *Wolf* may be a clue to give us a start, it sounds kinda gothic. Do you see any other words?"

"I can see *castle*."

"Let's see." Jules wrote down a couple more words, then stood back. "The castle of wolf something," she said, smiling.

"Yes, Wolfenbach, you have it Jules!"

"The castle of Wolfenbach, was that one of the horrid novels?"

"It was indeed," said George, turning to look at the library shelves, "and Count Wolfenbach locked his wife in the castle tower."

"Really? I thought Charlotte Brontë made that up."

"Long history of wives locked in towers I'm afraid."

"Okay, well at least we have one. Do you remember the other horrid novels?"

They looked at the anagrams to see if they could make them out. They deciphered *derisory hermits* as *Horrid Mysteries* and then George began to look again at the library shelves.

"Okay, this part is all history, art and encyclopaedia." He moved to the books either side of the door. "Quite a bit on flora and fauna, a few novels down here on the bottom shelves, Defoe and aha!" With a flourish, he pulled a large blue hardback out and held it up to the lamplight. "Yes, *The Castle of Wolfenbach*." He handed it to Jules who flicked through the first few pages and placed it on the desk. "No clues in here. See if you can find *Horrid Mysteries*."

Looking on the equivalent shelf on the right side of the door, George quickly found the book, a smaller novel bound in red leather. "*Horrid Mysteries* by Carl Friedrich August Grosse. Here you go. Any luck with the other anagrams?"

"No, see if you recognise any more titles."

"Good idea." George took a lamp and waved it across the shelves. "I don't suppose … Jules what was the last one?"

"Demitri housefly photos."

"Right. Just a moment, let's see over here." On the right corner of the shelf, George saw a title he recognised. "Does *The Mysteries of Udolpho* fit?"

Jules looked down at the parchment. "Yes! That's it, just one more to find, well done …"

She was unable to finish the sentence. As George pulled the large brown leather book from the shelf, their virtual world disappeared.

Eleven

Northanger Abbey, Part Two

"Conquer such whims and endeavour to strengthen your mind,"

As George's eyes adjusted to the brightness of the light, he raised his hand to shelter his face and looked around. He was standing in a meadow of long field grasses and herbs. His clothes looked formal, long black leather boots and deep blue trousers. Looking up he saw Jules, who was regarding her own dress, smiling and blinking in the sunlight. She looked very handsome in a medieval sage-green dress, fitted close at the waist and flowing in long folds to her feet.

"Well look at you," he said, "a lady again. And the sun's shining. Happy now?"

"Yes!" said Jules. "It's lovely. Wow, you have a

ruff! Bet you've never worn a lacy ruff before. Do you know where we are?"

George took in the whole view. The sun was high in the sky over the curl of a sparkling river at the foot of the meadow. At the top of the meadow was a terraced garden with palm trees and stone seats and beyond, a turreted castle. The hills were fringed with pine trees and green swathes like napkins, dotted with sheep.

"We came here when I touched the Udolpho book. I don't have a clue if this is it. Have you read it?"

"No, I haven't. Catherine talks about it so much in Northanger Abbey, I was curious. I asked Aphra to give me an outline. It's set in Gascony, a chateau, a naïve young heroine, a dastardly Italian villain, you know."

"This looks right for the south of France. Is there a boat house in it?" He pointed towards the edge of the lake where a small wooden cabin sat prettily on the shore.

"There is, we should check it out. By the way, the heroine is called Emily St Aubert. Do you think we're characters from the novel, extras, locals?"

"Could be. Pretty name." He paused for a second, admiring the scenery again. "Chateau or boat house. You choose."

"Well I'm as a happy as a clam in this sunshine and I'm done with spooky castles for now. Let's take a walk."

They strolled through the meadow, enjoying the lush grasses and purple hues of the flowers. At the river's edge, they paused to listen as the wavelets splashed gently on the bank. The river wound through the

116

landscape, spilling out through reed beds and on towards the plains. Over the low murmurs of the river, George thought he could hear a stringed melody, like a harp or guitar.

"Jules, can you hear that?"

"Yes, it's coming from the cabin I think."

They walked around to the door, which was open. The melody was coming from within, now accompanied by a young woman's voice singing a delicate air.

Jules knocked on the door. "Hello? Anyone there?"

The music stopped. Jules moved into the cabin, the light dimming, sunbeams criss-crossing the slatted floor. In the corner of the room was a young woman, seated on a wooden bench, holding a lute. Her long auburn hair was swept back and held with a blue ribbon, matching her simple French-blue dress.

"Hello, may we speak with you?"

"Pardon madame, qui etes vous?"

"Oh, you're French, of course you are. Excusez-moi mademoiselle, parlez-vous Anglais? Vous etes Emily n'est-ce pas?"

"Oui, yes, I am Emily. I speak some English. And you are?"

"My name is Jules and this is George. From the village, we're touring the area, for the landscapes …"

Emily stood up and held out her hand. Jules shook it warmly and George stepped forward, taking her hand in turn. "Enchanté," said Emily, taking her lute and leading the way to the door. "Please let me show you my father's estate." Standing outside the boat house, Emily described the landscape in rapturous tones, pointing out a pair of curlews, her favourite mountain ash trees, the shepherds' huts dotting the slopes of the valley, the gently flowing river and its inhabitants.

"Thank you mademoiselle, you are passionate about the beauty in this valley."

"Oh yes," said Emily, colouring a little. "The poetry of the valley is dear to us." She raised her head to the hills and spoke in full voice -

"Down yonder glade, two lovers steal, to shun the fairy queen.

Who frowns upon their plighted vows, and jealous is of me."

She turned back to them.

"I also write songs to play on my lute. Papa loves to hear them."

"You sing like an angel," said Jules. "We won't disturb you any longer. Should we walk up to the chateau do you think, or along the river?"

"Oh, if you please, I think you should take a boat and enjoy the river. On a day like today, you may see swallows and flycatchers, there is a rowing boat you can use." Emily pointed to a bank to the right of the boat house, sheltered by the reeds. "Please, enjoy."

"Thank you," said George, "you are very kind."

"Merci mademoiselle." Jules gave a little bow and they walked down to the rowing boat.

As George untied the boat, Jules noticed a card on the seat at the back. "We have a clue," she said, waving the card at George. "Should I row or do you think you can handle it?"

"Allow me, madame," said George, settling into the

middle seat and grasping the oars. Jules sat in the back seat and smiled. "This is fun."

"So it is. Go on then, read it out while I try this. I rowed at college a few times, surprisingly enough I was pretty good!"

Jules read aloud from the card:

To play your parts in Emma, you have only to solve this riddle. I am an English novel, written in 1847. Make your peace with a carnival of characters, a stop along the pilgrim's route. Time is short, be sharp about it.

"Okay," said George, nudging the boat away from the bank with an oar, "early Victorian, sounds like it might be Dickens, a carnival of characters? David Copperfield maybe?"

Jules looked across at a willow tree, dipping its branches in the flowing water and exhaled slowly, turning her head to the sun. "I hope we can solve it, I would love a part in Emma." She glanced again at the card. "What's this about *make your peace*, I don't get that. *Time is short*, I guess we only have a half hour, but that's just the usual time, right?"

"Let's drift a minute, have a think." George pulled in the oars and they floated with the current, caressed by the warm breeze and scattered birdcalls.

"I think I can make my peace with this," said George, "it's wonderful. How about George Eliot or Thomas Hardy? I don't suppose you would call their novels a carnival of characters though."

Jules sat up straight, ran her hand through the water

and flicked a handful at George. "Nice try," he said laughing, "if only I could feel my face!"

Jules splashed him again and he dipped the left oar sending a cascade of water over her legs. "Okay, I give up!" she laughed. "Let's think, Victorian novelists, pilgrims … Trollope, or Wilkie Collins, one of the Brontës?"

They drifted a little further downstream, closing their eyes, letting their minds drift over parades of characters, pilgrims and carnivals.

"George, did you say make peace? Is that it? Quite simple if it is. William Makepeace Thackeray. Vanity Fair!"

"Yes! said George, "look sharp, *Becky Sharp*. I'd forgotten about Vanity Fair. That fits exactly."

They drifted for a few minutes enjoying the peace until reluctantly they felt that it was time to return. George turned the boat, holding one of the oars in the current and paddling with the other. He then pulled harder and the boat moved back upstream towards the cabin.

"George, I'm sorry about your library troubles, I hope it isn't as bad as it sounds."

"Thanks Jules, frankly I don't know what to make of it all. On the one hand, here we are taking part in a technological marvel of virtual reality, whilst back in the real world there seems to be no obvious way of funding the library. We do have some ideas though, I'd like to talk them through with you, maybe on Monday?"

"Sure, happy to help any way we can."

The boat bumped softly into the river bank and they

jumped out. Emily was waiting for them outside the boat house. "I hope your voyage was enjoyable?" she asked.

"It was awesome, thanks Emily."

On the side of the cabin, a green exit sign had appeared. George nudged Jules and they said their farewells to Emily. As they turned to go, Jules stopped. "One more thing. Watch out for strange Italian aristocrats, they can be very dangerous." Emily looked impassively back at her, shrugged her shoulders and waved. "Of course, Madame, I will do my best. Au revoir."

Jules reached for George's hand and led them through the door.

Twelve

Schrodinger's cat

"Dad!"

"Hello George, it's so good to see you." George's father was waiting for him in the apartment when he walked through the door. He wrapped George in a hug and they went through to the sitting room where Uncle Jack and Jax were playing Scrabble at the table.

"Hello everyone, it's lovely to have a house full. Do you all have drinks? Having fun Jax?" George gave her a hug and went to change.

It was a chilly afternoon. George had left work early after his father had said he would be over for the evening, on his way to a psychology conference at the university. Jack and Arthur took over the kitchen and after a great deal of noisy clattering, flour dust and delicious baking aromas, they produced marguerite pizzas, salad and ginger beer. The discussions were lively, Arthur describing his forthcoming lecture and Jack interjecting with questions and anecdotes. George mainly listened, enjoying the distraction, watching his father's enthusiasm for his work.

"So," concluded Arthur, "the last time I asked for questions from the audience, one smart young thing stood up and said, "do you think your theory works like Schrodinger's cat?" Jack and George laughed and Jax, who was rearranging the Scrabble tiles asked, "who's Schrodinger's cat?"

Arthur reached over and tousled Jax's blond hair. "That," he said "would have made an excellent answer. Mr Schrodinger was a scientist. He lived for a while in Zurich and if you visit his old house you'll see a life-sized cat figure around the grounds, but no visitor knows in advance where it will be. They're having a bit of laugh about his cat theory. You see Jax, he and Einstein were talking about quantum physics. In their idea, a cat in box with a radioactive substance could be both dead and alive at the same time."

"That's silly!" said Jax, giggling.

"Yes it is," replied Arthur, "Schrodinger said that himself. He was trying to show how absurd some quantum theories sounded at the time, about a century ago."

"But," said George, "these days people still use the idea to show that sometimes, two things can be true at the same time, even if they seem to contradict each other."

"Like this pizza then," said Jax. "It's yummy hot and I don't want it to get cold. But it will be just as yummy in the morning."

"Yes!" said Arthur, chuckling. "I'll remember that

for the next question time."

Jack and Jax cleared away the plates and went to the kitchen to tidy up. George and Arthur sat in the armchairs and watched the clouds scudding across the sky, leaving the cathedral in a rain-soaked impressionist grey.

"Time isn't straight you know George."

George frowned, trying to see his father's point. He shrugged. "You mean it's curved? I know that, at least I think I do."

"Yes, but it's also flexible. We tend to see events in the past as fixed in time. But that's just our way of filing them in our memories and trying to make sense of the world. At the smallest level, it's just particles swishing away in nature. That's what I find so comforting about those clouds and that sky. The sky doesn't worry about time; clouds gather, it rains, the sky clears, the sun sends light photons down to warm up planet earth. There's a group of people in the Amazon who don't measure time at all, in fact they have no past tense in their language. Everything is in the present for them. "

"Oh, the grand scheme of things. A wider perspective."

"Yes, but also the way our minds react. If you spend a day in a forest, you start to feel part of it. Your mind starts to settle, like sand in an hourglass. It can feel as if time is standing still. Nature, art and love, those are fundamental to humans and they are essentially timeless."

"Are you turning into a hippy Dad?"

Arthur grinned. "No, just tossing a few ideas out,

seeing how they land."

"Okay, thanks Dad. It's always good to try a new perspective. Uncle Jack's been saying the same. I do hope your lecture goes well. And I hope you don't have to field any tricky questions on Schrodinger's cat!"

There was a knock on the door and few seconds later Emily appeared to collect Jax. "Hello George, oh hello Arthur, it's good to see you. How are you and Clare?"

"We're fine, thanks Emily, it's good to see you too."

Emily smiled, "goodness, it smells of warm pizza in here."

George stood up and walked over. "It was delicious. Let's go and see if Jax has left you any."

Late on Wednesday afternoon, George was setting out a display of brightly-coloured fiction books to tempt passing readers near the counter. As he was finishing up, his phone rang. There were no readers on the ground floor so he took the call at the desk.

"Hey George, how are you feeling after our last time travel?"

"Jules, hi, it was … educational I thought. It gave me a new perspective on Northanger Abbey. You?"

"Excellent. Great to be out on the river too. I like how they change it up, different characters, situations, challenges. Can't wait to see what they do with Emma. By the way, did you read the terms and conditions they mailed us? I thought it was all pretty vanilla. Standard user terms and a load of lawyer talk."

"Exactly Jules, I couldn't see anything in it. The Knightley corporation is just a shell company by the looks of it. Bertie couldn't find anything official. And only two more adventures, as far as we know. We might as well play our part and enjoy it while it lasts."

"Agreed, no point over-thinking it. I haven't had any headaches or motion sickness like we used to have with virtual reality. I'm sleeping okay too. Happy to stay in the game as long as you are. Any news on your library funding?"

"No, nothing I'm afraid. The Professor has arranged a meeting for us in a couple of weeks, that's all. We're chasing our tails here."

"Just don't give up George. I'm sending you some ideas, but don't bet the farm on them okay?"

"Thanks Jules, will do. How are the history quizzes going down with the students there?"

"They're great George, thanks for sending them. The younger kids loved all that Henry the eighth stuff, especially when they could interview Henry on tv. They gave him a pretty tough time!"

George cycled slowly back round the cathedral to the apartment, thoughts and ideas running through his mind like the high horsetail clouds above him. He rather enjoyed the image described by his father. "You aren't responsible for your thoughts," he had said, "just watch them passing, allow them to disperse and watch the next one. It's like a meditation."

Finding himself alone in the apartment, he finished reading *The Battle of Britain* over a bowl of noodle soup. As he made a pot of Assam tea, Bertie updated him on the news and events.

"You have appointments next week for your annual check-up and the dentist to seed your new tooth. I will remind you the day before. Your mother rang, I told her you would call her later. Jack said he'll be back tomorrow. He said he had to see a man about a dog. Will you be having a dog sir?"

George laughed. "Certainly not, Bertie, I think he meant he was off on one of his missions. Could you arrange for some flowers to be sent to Jules for her birthday? If you could show me some autumn bouquets on the screen, I'll pick one later."

"Yes sir."

George stood at the window sipping his tea and watching the light fade over the autumn-red hues of the trees. Walking over to his corner desk, he took out a manila envelope and withdrew Emily's handwritten letter from the previous year. Glancing at it and shaking his head, he opened the balcony door. There was a light wind and a soft glow in the dusky evening light. Very deliberately, he tore the letter into pieces, smaller and smaller until a little pile was left on the metal coffee table. Out of the corner of his eye, he saw a flash of green and Squawk landed on the rail, twitching his tail. A few seconds later a second magpie dropped silently next to Squawk, a bright blue stripe on its nose. "Hello Squawk, who's your friend?" said George, reaching for some sunflower seeds. He spread some on the rail and the magpies tapped away at them like a pair of woodpeckers.

"Okay my feathered friends, I have an idea, see what you think." He gathered the letter fragments in his right hand, leant back and threw them into the wind as far as he could. A gust caught them and they blew high into the cool air, spreading like tiny snowflakes. The two magpies appeared unmoved. They carried on scattering the seeds with their beaks. "Enjoy your evening," said George, giving the birds a wave and quietly closing the door.

Thirteen

Bats in the belfry

"George, sorry to disturb, there's a chap to see you."

Anne was standing at the top of the stairs carrying a screen tablet in one hand and a scanner in the other. "He said he's from Natural England."

"Thanks Anne, I'll pop down." George was sitting at his desk next to Roxie, studying some rather tatty-looking sepia maps. They were looking for evidence of pirates.

"Did he say Natural England?" said Roxie.

"I think so."

"That's great!" Roxie clapped her hands in glee, raising a none-too-impressed look from an elderly man with his nose in a large textbook.

"You know about this?" asked George.

"Oh yes, me and Jim, you remember Jim? We've been checking out your furry creatures on the roof. We think they're bats, so Jim called Natural England to come and have a look. Didn't want to worry you about it George - Jim thought maybe they wouldn't even bother to come. But they have, isn't that amazing?"

"Ah, yes, I suppose so," said George, wondering if there might be a large bill attached if they had to start a shelter for rare bats. "I think we'll have to come back to these maps, I can't read the text, we need to magnify it. We'll scan them in and see if it's what you're after. Do you want to come and meet the bat fellow?"

"Do I? Of course, let's go! It's just a shame Jim isn't here, wait till I tell him."

They walked down to the reception desk to find a tall man in his mid-twenties with spiky dark hair, red cheeks and an oversized fleece jacket with a *Natural England* logo on one side. He was carrying a baseball cap and a small canvas holdall.

"Hello, I'm George Sanders, and this is Roxie." George held out his hand.

The man smiled broadly and shook George's hand vigorously and then Roxie's. "Robin Goodfellow, Natural England, nice to meet you both." He looked around approvingly. "Fab place you have here, eighteenth century? Original windows. Brilliant."

"So, you've come about some bats?" ventured George, not exactly sure what to say. "It was Jim, Roxie's friend, he contacted you?"

"Yes, yes, exactly," said Robin, a local burr coming through in his voice. "Course, they might not be bats, eh? Might be something else entirely."

"Quite. Well, where would you like to look Robin?"

"If you have a roof access, that would be perfect."

"Right, follow me. The access is in the store room on the second floor. We don't go up there usually, it is ventilated but we don't store books in there - it's not safe for staff."

They trooped up to the second floor and into the store room behind the counter. At the back of the room there was a wooden ladder folded against the wall and a white roof hatch in the ceiling above.

"Do you need anything from us Robin? Cup of tea? There is one light, but you'll need a torch."

"Thank you no, I have everything here." He tapped his bag and placed it next to the ladder. "A cup of tea in ten minutes would be magic."

George put the kettle on in the staff room and they waited while Robin made his way tentatively up into the roof space.

A few minutes later, George came back with the tea. A smiling upside down face appeared out of the hatch. "Nearly finished, just need to take some samples, okay?"

"Samples?" asked George.

"Droppings," said Robin, ducking back into the roof space, "won't be a minute."

Slowly sipping his tea, George felt unreasonably nervous, waiting for the verdict. Roxie was sitting on an old tea crate, leafing through a bound set of fashion prints from the nineteen-twenties.

"Take it easy there George, you know this may be good for the library."

"How, exactly?"

"If you have rare bats, you could apply for a grant to

modify the building. I looked it up."

"Well, silver linings, I suppose Roxie." He thought about the Professor and his idea of selling the building. Good luck with that, if we have to sell it with roosting tenants!

There was a creaking noise from the ceiling above them. They both looked up. Suddenly there was a crash, the sound of wood splintering and a black-booted leg appeared through the ceiling followed by a cloud of dust and a muffled shout of "dammit, dammit, you idiot. Ow!" They jumped up and stood below the hole and the swinging boot.

"Are you okay?" shouted George.

"Ah, ow, yeah, I think so," said Robin. "Give me a sec. Ow. Yep, there we go."

The boot drew back into the ceiling. After more scraping, creaking wood and dust, Robin's feet appeared on the ladder and he climbed gingerly down, shaking his head. He sat down heavily on a box.

"I am really sorry," he said, still shaking his head.

"Don't worry," said George, handing him a mug of tea, "drink that and rest for a minute."

"Thanks." Robin sipped his tea thoughtfully, then rubbed his right knee. "Bit sore."

"Would you like us to call anyone?" asked George.

"No, thanks, it'll mend. Listen, I know a chap who can fix that for you, cheap as chips. I expect my boss will pay, he owes me a couple of favours."

"Okay, well it could have been worse."

"Yeah," said Robin, grinning ruefully, "I suppose it could."

"So … did you find any, er … droppings?"

"Oh, yes, I did. Better than that, I actually saw a couple of bats, right at the top of the eaves. Beautiful. Barbastelle, if I'm not mistaken, looks like Jim was right."

"Wow," said Roxie.

"*Barbastellus barbastellus*," said Robin. "The name comes from that sort of beardy look they have around their chin - quite unusual around here. This is their mating season, that's why you've seen them flying around the roof."

"So what happens now?" asked George.

"Well, not much for the moment," said Robin, "as they're so active. They shouldn't be disturbed. You can still access the roof for maintenance, but please be careful. I'll get my mate to sort that hole with some two by two and a bit of plaster, should be fine." He drank down the rest of his tea and handed the cup to George. "Thanks for that. Now, I'll write my report and I expect you'll have a couple of visits to look at bat numbers, put up a camera, that sort of thing. Then in the spring they'll make a plan of how to look after the roost."

George was quite relieved by this. "Thanks for coming Robin, we'll look forward to reading your report."

"You made *my* day for sure," said Roxie, grinning. "I hope the knee's okay."

They made their way slowly back to reception, saw Robin out and told Anne all about the newest residents of Whirligig Lane.

"Bats," my goodness," said Anne. "So that chap

Robin, he was the bat man. Maybe he should have a sidekick, you know, to keep him out of trouble." She giggled, winking at Roxie.

"Anne! I thought I made all the corny jokes around here," said George. "Right then Roxie, shall we get back to the unreadable maps and the pirates?"

"Lead the way Captain George."

Fourteen

Emma

"If I loved you less, I might be able to talk about it more."

When George arrived at Whirligig Lane on Friday morning, he found a copy of Jane Austen's *Emma* on his desk. It was a small hardback with a deep blue leather cover and gold lettering. George turned it over in his hand, admiring the tooling and opened it, feeling the quality of the paper and checking the date of publication. Coming to the title page he found an ivory card with the following message:

Miss Austen invites you to take your part in a scene from Emma. You will play Mr Frank Churchill. The scene is volume two, chapter eight. Jules will play the part of Miss Emma Woodhouse. Endeavour is more important than accuracy. A successful performance will gain you entrance to the final adventure, Pride and Prejudice.

George sat back and turned the card in his fingers. Frank Churchill and Emma! Better do some homework before tomorrow evening. He flicked to volume two in the book and found chapter eight. Smiling, he reached for his phone and sent a message to Jules.

At the end of a quiet morning of cataloguing and shelving, George looked at the clock, the weather and his cheese sandwich. Time for a change. He popped the sandwich in the fridge, said goodbye to Anne and headed out into the hazy sunshine of the cathedral green. He turned away from the cathedral and took a gentle stroll around the square, squinting in The Old Curiosity Bookshop window, nodding at familiar faces and finally settling at a wooden table outside the Crooked Chimney Café. It was famous for its soups, served in a scooped-out roll of crusty bread which slowly softened. He chose fresh tomato and basil and pulled a battered paperback copy of *Moby Dick* out of his back pack. He was determined to finish it, even though Melville's style was like a Dickens at sea, full of colourful characters and imagery, but rather long and meandering. The fearsome eponymous whale didn't even make an appearance until the second half of the book. There she blows! Nevertheless, he had enjoyed plunging headlong into the story, joining Ishmael, Queequeg and Captain Ahab in their epic voyage.

A shadow fell over the table and he looked up. "Hello George, enjoying the sunshine?" Kamal stood by the table, sheltering his eyes. "Do you have a moment?"

"Hi Kamal, yes, of course, grab a chair, would you like a drink?"

"No, thanks, I'm not stopping. I just wanted to thank you for talking to my supervisor. She invited me in for a chat, listened to what I had to say and they're allowing my commercial work, as long as my report is handed in by next summer. It's an extra three months. I think they were concerned that I would ask for a year's extension or something. She called it *the dreaded curse of the never-ending Phd.* I promised her it would be on time."

"That's good. Do the finances work out for you now?"

"Yes, I think so. I have two tech projects which are nearly finished. One will be completed next week actually." He leaned across the table and said in a quiet voice: "and by the way, I do like Jane Austen. Thanks for your help." He winked, turned on his heel and strode away across the square.

"Wait, what? Kamal!" But George was too late. Kamal's receding figure was obscured by a crowd of chattering tourists.

"Bertie, call Jules please, on screen."

"Yes sir."

Jules was cycling, clad head to foot in light grey lycra, her hair tied back and beads of sweat on her forehead. "Hey George, give me a second, just winding down from a ten miler."

"Wow, take your time, are you in the garage?" Jules hopped off the exercise bike and grabbed a towel.

"Yup, new bike. We put it out here for now as it's cooler, but I think we'll move it upstairs in the winter. I like it, it's way more fun racing against other guys than pumping out the miles on your own."

"Very true. I do like the fresh air though, the sun on my back. So, did your invitation arrive?"

"Yeah, someone left it on my desk inside a copy of Emma. Nice little hardback. You learning your lines?"

"A little, but the card said we don't need to be accurate. Endeavour is more important. I'll take them at their word on that."

"One thing," said Jules, taking her phone and perching on a work bench. "I'm real glad they didn't put us in the scene where Mr Elton makes violent love to Emma in the coach. No offence George."

George laughed. "None taken. It could have been rather embarrassing. I remember our English teacher at school telling us not to take it literally. It's just verbal love making. We all had a good snigger about that I can tell you. Birthday girl tomorrow aren't you?"

"Yes, twenty-nine again. I wish!"

"Patrick taking you anywhere special?"

"Oh yeah, lunch at The Old Seasalt Grill overlooking the marina. It's beautiful, we had local oysters last time and sat there all evening watching the world go by."

"Sounds fabulous. I'll join you in spirit and toast you with a glass of Grenache, even though I can't quite see you across the Atlantic. I wish I could be there."

"You'll have to jet over one of these days, the superfast is only two hours now. Save up and come for a long weekend." She stood up and shook out her hair. "Okay, I have to shower, I guess the next time I see you I'll be Emma Woodhouse. You know what? I'm a little nervous!"

"Surely not. Well I'm looking forward to it. Frank Churchill is a fun character and I hope to do him justice. Do you remember how he rides sixteen miles for a haircut?"

"I do. And how he keeps his secret for half the book. By the way, do you know who did a review of *Emma* when it was first published?"

"No. Who?"

"Sir Walter Scott. He loved it! See you in Highbury George."

George performed a final read-through of the scene in Emma, jumped up and grabbed his jacket from the hall. He was about to open the front door when Uncle Jack came out of his bedroom. He was dressed as a vicar.

"Off to a party, Uncle Jack? It's quite late."

"Funeral."

"Oh, goodness, I'm sorry, who …?"

"I don't know who it was."

George looked at Jack uncomprehendingly. "You didn't know the person?"

Jack reached for his flat cap and held the door open for George. "I'm doing a memorial in a boat off the beach in Lyme Regis.   The family asked for me personally, that was nice."

"Oh, right, well that explains it."   George was used to Jack's eccentric ways but was quite unaware that he was an ordained member of the clergy.

"I got my licence last year.   It's been quite a headscratcher to be honest Georgie.   Never thought of myself as spiritual, but the people in Cuba, they have a sort of way with their religion, it's hard to explain.   It changed me.   Long story short, my friend Clara asked if I could say some words as they scattered her father's ashes in the ocean.   Turns out I was good at it.   So we're off to Lyme to give a proper send off to someone I never knew, who was loved by many people and will be missed by many more."

"Right, well I hope it all goes … respectfully."

"Me too.   See you in a couple of days Georgie."

Miss Austen materialised in front of the bookcase.   Her hair glowed in the moonlight filtering softly through the windows.

"Good evening George"

"Good evening Miss Austen."

"Are you prepared to play your part?"

"As ready as I'll ever be!"

"Very good.   Before we begin, could you please tell me why Emma is your favourite of my novels?"

"Yes, of course."   George thought for a moment. "Just a minute, I don't recall discussing that with you.

Have you been listening in on my conversations?"

The figure was silent for a few seconds. "Our knowledge comes from many sources."

"I'm not sure if that's polite, or ethical come to that." George waited for Miss Austen to speak. She was silent until George answered her question.

"Okay, moving swiftly on. Why is *Emma* my favourite? It's quite simple really: it's the intimacy, the personal detail, the world in miniature." He paused, looking at the figure in front of him, taking in the details of her face. "As a reader you see what's happening through different eyes, not just through Emma's. You may not be aware of all the perspectives whilst the story unfolds, but it's immensely satisfying to see how it all plays out. Emma is one of the first unreliable narrators and for me, that makes the story very modern. She's the most fascinating, naïve, fallible, completely human person. I adore her. She is, as you so beautifully remarked in the novel, *faultless, despite all her faults*."

"Thank you George. Or should I say Frank? I am looking forward to the soiree at the Coles' house. I will be watching you."

George lifted the visor to his face and covered his eyes. "Let's go then."

The white screen faded to reveal a large drawing room, brightly lit by candelabras and a glowing fire. The room was ostentatiously comfortable, with ivory sofas, long aquamarine drapes at the windows, Romanesque rugs and mahogany wing chairs.

George was standing next to the white marble fireplace. On his left was a sofa and seated, two elegant young blonde ladies who should be none other than Miss Emma Woodhouse and Miss Harriet Smith. Across the room he could see other ladies including one, tall with dark eyelashes and eyebrows, her irregular beauty conspicuous in the company. Jane Fairfax perhaps? He moved away from the fire and stood in front of the lady on the sofa. She looked up at him, smiled and winked. It was Jules, her face perfectly matched into a graceful Emma. She wore a silk rose dress with puffed sleeves and lace around the neck, the high collar framing her oval face and dimpled chin.

"Mr Churchill," said Jules, rising, "may I introduce Miss Harriet Smith. Harriet, this is Mr Frank Churchill." George bowed to them both. "I am delighted to make your acquaintance Miss Smith, I have heard so much about you from your good friend."

"You are the first gentleman to join us Mr Churchill," said Jules. "Are the others so wrapped in their enjoyment of their cigars and parish matters that they cannot remember us?"

"I confess that I am always impatient to leave the dining room. Not only for the superior company, you understand. I just cannot stand to sit long, I would rather walk, talk or dance indeed!"

"Well, now that you are here, perhaps you might tell myself and Miss Smith some tales of your home in Yorkshire. Enscombe is the place, is it not?"

"I would be glad to, if there were much to tell. Sadly, my Aunt is disinclined to company in the evenings, despite the many invitations from the great families in the area. The town is small and very quiet.

For my part, I am hard put to negotiate an evening out or an acquaintance to stay for the night. I wished very much to travel abroad last year, but could not persuade my Aunt to it. I should not complain, however, as my aunt and uncle are supportive in their own way. On reflection, I find that my travels to Highbury are a perfect substitute. But my visit is half over already! How the time flies when one is in good company."

"Indeed." Jules fixed George with an amused stare and a raised eyebrow. "Although you did find time to travel all the way to town for a haircut."

George laughed. "Touché Miss Woodhouse. I cannot regret it however; a true gentleman must have a mind to his appearance."

He looked across the room as the other gentlemen came into the drawing room. This was his cue to cross the room and join Jane Fairfax. He tried to catch her eye, succeeded and then remarked to Emma: "those curls! Is this an Irish fashion, or some idea of her own? I must ask her about it, if you will excuse me Miss Woodhouse."

"Yes, of course." Jules inclined her head and sat back down on the sofa with Harriet. George crossed the room, nodding to an upright, tall gentleman who was watching him with hawk-like disapproval. He stood in front of Miss Fairfax, wondering if the conversation he had prepared would serve, leant in close and said softly, "Jane, you look enchanting. Are you enjoying your evening?"

"Frank!" she whispered, "be quiet, have you no discretion?"

"Aye, plenty! But I choose not to use it this evening. I have had enough of pretence and subterfuge."

"Then," said Jane, "I must be a conscience for both of us. You endanger our arrangement with your flirtations, especially with Miss Woodhouse. You embarrass me and you embarrass yourself sir."

George sighed. "I am sorry Jane, I thought it the best diversion."

Jane looked over his shoulder at the other guests and her cheeks glowed. "Please Frank, will you behave as a gentleman should? For my sake."

George nodded and placed himself beside her, so that he could observe the rest of the party. Jules was deep in conversation with Mrs Weston. That was good, their conversation would run far and wide, including Mrs Weston's idea that Mr Knightley may be in love with Jane Fairfax. Mrs Weston would promote the idea with enthusiasm. Jules, as Emma, would pour as much cold water on the idea as she could. George smiled at the thought. A few minutes later he saw Mr Cole approaching Jules and knew that he was expected to join him in entreating her to play the pianoforte.

Jules needed little persuasion. She nodded graciously and walked over to the Broadwood piano which sat majestically in front of the drapes. George followed her and took up a position near the windows. Seating herself, Jules looked at the first piece of music on the stand. It was an unfamiliar waltz. She cleared her throat and turned it over to reveal the next. *An English Country Garden*. That would be fine.

She placed her hands to play the opening *G* chord

and stopped, startled. The piano had started before she touched the keys. It was playing itself! The opening bars rang out as her hands hovered over the keyboard. She looked at George quizzically and he responded with a shrug and a broad grin as he understood what was happening. The scene was clearly designed so that people with no musical ability could join in. Jules waited for the next bar, took a deep breath and started to sing, observing with some satisfaction as the gentlemen smiled and the ladies tapped their fans. George joined in for the chorus whilst Jules moved her hands enthusiastically up and down the keyboard without touching it. George had a decent enough singing voice, but quality was less important than a show, he felt. He raised his hands and tried to project his voice as Emily had coached him, somewhat unsuccessfully he had to admit. The song came to an end, the guests applauding politely. Jules looked across at him; a second song was expected. He nodded, reaching in to turn the page. He hoped that the next piece would be another simple song. *Scarborough Fair*. Well at least he knew it!

Their singing performance was unassuming at first, improving towards the end and attracted admiring glances from the assembly. As the guests applauded, Jules leant in towards George and said: "that's enough of that. I think it's Jane's turn."

Jane Fairfax obliged, George accompanying her singing as well as he could. He noticed that she touched the keys very gently, closed her eyes and played as if the music had completely enveloped her. She played a second but her voice began to strain during the coda. He saw the tall gentleman talking to Miss Bates and looking across at the piano with a serious expression. That would be Mr Knightley, trying to rescue Jane Fairfax from taxing her voice and from the tiresome exertions of Frank Churchill.

Miss Bates did intervene and Miss Fairfax was allowed to retire gracefully from the pianoforte, her duty admirably accomplished.

Jules was visibly relieved and more relaxed now that the singing was past. She sat back on the sofa next to Harriet who beamed at her and patted her arm. They watched as the butler and two maids appeared and proceeded to clear a space for dancing.

Shortly afterwards, Mrs Weston took over the piano and couples started to form for the first dance. George addressed himself formally to Jules and offered his hand. "Miss Woodhouse, would you honour me with your hand for the first and second?"

She smiled and stood. "Of course Mr Churchill, please lead the way." They walked through the other couples to the head of the dance, near the piano. Mrs Weston struck up a jolly waltz and the couples formed for quadrilles. George had been wondering how he would be able to complete any formal dance moves as an avatar. He had expected to simply follow the other dancers and walk around, hoping that nobody would be judging the lack of actual dancing. As the first reel began, no such problem arose. His avatar took over and danced for him! Back in the library, his gloved hands were no longer controlling his movement; the dance was running itself. George looked at Jules as their hands met in the passing twirls, her rose dress swaying in time to the music and her diamond necklace reflecting the candlelight. Her eyes met his and together they laughed.

A second dance followed and too soon it was over. The couples promenaded around the room for the last time and began their goodbyes to Mr and Mrs Coles.

"That was fun George!" said Jules as they stood in a quiet alcove watching the guests mill around, their spirits still high and cheeks glowing. "Like a two hundred year old school prom."

"Very good," said George, "I wonder if we passed? As it turned out, we didn't have to play or dance at all. I like the way that's designed, anyone can join in, even a duffer like me!"

A black-suited butler approached them from the drawing room door.

"Watch out George, butler alert!"

"Okay, keep calm, I've got your back."

"That's reassuring," said Jules, moving closer to him.

"Sir, madam," said the butler, "the carriages are ready."

"Splendid, lead on!" said George and they followed the butler to the front door of the house where the remaining guests were waiting, shaking hands and saying their goodbyes. George stood next to the Westons whilst Jules joined Harriett to wait for James, their driver.

A dark carriage drew up, its large wooden wheels crunching on the gravel. The butler stepped forward to open the door. He beckoned George and Jules over and invited them to step inside. George noticed a green light above the carriage door and pointed it out to Jules, who accepted his offered arm and climbed in. He followed, expecting the butler to close the door. Instead, the butler climbed in, settled himself in the seat opposite theirs and took a small black leather folio from inside his waistcoat.

"Okay buster, what's your game?" Jules had clearly had enough of men in penguin suits telling her what to do.

The butler paused, looked at them both and said: "your task is complete, but you have not yet received your marks."

"Our marks, really?"

"Yes madam."

Jules sighed, looked at George and nodded. "I guess that would be okay."

"Sir," he said, looking at George, "your acting was judged as first class, your singing as average."

George started chuckling and nodded to Jules. "Beat that!"

The butler turned to Jules. "Madam, your acting was judged as first class, your singing as very good. Congratulations to you both, you are successful." Without another word, he opened the carriage door and stepped out. A green light appeared above the opposite carriage door.

"Awesome!" said Jules. "So that's it, we just leave out the door?"

"I suppose so," said George, "rather inelegant,

wouldn't you say?"

Jules sighed. "You know, I'm going to miss these Saturday evenings."

"Definitely. The real world is highly overrated."

"Chin up soldier. Call me next week."

"Will do." George offered his hand, they opened the door and stepped out.

Fifteen

"Lord, what fools these mortals be!"

"Ah George, how are you?"

Professor Dobbs peered through a gap in the bookshelves like a hungry horse in search of fodder. George was on his knees, rearranging the fiction shelves on the second floor, dusting the books and placing aside those volumes which were overdue some care and repair.

"Hello Professor." He stood up, brushing the dust off his knees. "I'm okay thanks, how are you?"

"Oh, very well, yes, yes." The professor came around the shelves into the bay where George was working. "Hmm, historical fiction, I see." He picked up a rather tatty brown copy of *Tess of the d'Urbervilles* and sniffed it. He turned up his nose and frowned, his eyebrows forming into a formidable grey hedge. "A very sad tale indeed, poor lass." He attempted a smile.

"Yes," said George, surprised by the Professor's comment. "It's very affecting for young people. Some are overwhelmed by the sense of injustice done to Tess. I know I was."

"Ah yes, of course, very affecting indeed." He put the book back on the pile. "I just wanted to see how the troops are, if any new ideas have been forthcoming so to speak. Initiatives, discussions, that sort of thing."

"We're doing our best, as you can imagine Professor." George was feeling impatient, wondering what the Professor was fishing for, waiting for him to come to the point.

"I … have to make a trip abroad for a week. To the US of A in fact. I thought I would let you know. Meeting some business partners."

"I hope you enjoy your trip," said George, picking up a Penguin classic paperback of *Great Expectations* and brushing the dust off the top.

"We have our meeting arranged for when I return. I think it will be time to come to some conclusions then."

"Right." said George.

"Well, keep up the good work, I'll see you in a week or so."

"Okay. Goodbye." George turned back to his work feeling like a rower who had just dropped his oar.

It was Monday midday. The October winds howled around the building, rattling the sashes and chasing the birds into the hedges. George was sitting at his first floor desk staring into a mug of hot chocolate.

"Wakey wakey," said Anne, dropping a letter onto the desk. "The builder's here to fix the ceiling. Handsome Raj is looking after him."

"Thanks," said George, "I'll take a look later."

"If you don't mind me saying," said Anne, "you look a bit fed up."

"Oh, no. I mean, I don't mind you saying. And you're right, I am rather fed up. It could be the weather." They both looked out at the grey clouds racing across the sky.

"I saw Emily yesterday," said Anne, tidying the magazines into a neat pile on the table. "She asked after us all."

"Oh, right," said George, putting down his mug. "Did she say anything else?"

"No, we were just passing the time of day, so to speak."

"I ... " George paused. "I think I'll check on the builder, make sure he doesn't put his foot through the ceiling."

"Good idea," said Anne.

As George gingerly pushed open the store room door, he saw an older man in white overalls sawing pieces of softwood on a work bench.

"Hello, said George, "I won't hold you up. Is there anything you need?"

"No thanks, the other chap made me tea. This shouldn't take long. I'll do the plaster board today and come back to skim it tomorrow."

"Great, thanks. Any sign of the bats?"

"No, very quiet up there. I had to move a couple of floorboards and it looks like someone left some old boxes up there. I put them next to the ladder." He pointed to two shallow brown cardboard boxes, creased and covered in dust. One was slightly ripped, revealing what looked like hardback books inside.

"Oh, thanks, I'll move them out of your way." George walked over and lifted the top box, intrigued by its shape and size. The man nodded, returning to his bench.

George took the boxes, one at a time down to the first floor and placed them carefully on the large table next to the window. He found the small vacuum, opened the window and gave them a quick clean. The lid on the first box was loose and George could see several books through the rent in the side. He removed the cardboard lid and set it aside. The books were all hardbacks, dark and light brown leather covers with black and maroon stripes on the spines showing the titles. They were evidently part of a set or had been rebound for a former owner. A shiver of excitement ran through George as he read the first titles:

Robinson Crusoe, Tristram Shandy, Oroonoko, Pilgrim's Progress, Gulliver's Travels.

He carefully removed each volume from the box and placed it on the table. There were sixteen in total. Underneath the books were several sheets of plain white

paper with a letter heading: *Beaton Cathedral library.*
George opened *Robinson Crusoe*, admiring the marbled
blue end papers and the fine condition. *The Life and
Strange Surprizing Adventures of Robinson Crusoe of
York, Mariner.* No author name, that was curious. What
would they do with them? They were good enough to
sell for a reasonable sum. Or should they be returned to
the Cathedral? George mulled over these questions
whilst he turned to the second box.

This one was slightly larger and sturdier, a thick
cardboard transit box with metal corners. The top was
secured with red cloth pieces tied around both sides.
George carefully loosened the cloths, pulled them away
and lifted the lid. A layer of canvas lay across the top
to protect the contents. He untucked it, drew it away
and revealed a single large folio book bound in dark
green leather. Gently lifting it out, he looked at the
spine and nearly dropped it. *Shakespeare's Plays.*

George exhaled softly and decided it was a good
time to sit down. He drew up a chair and pulled the book
towards him, feeling the soft calfskin cover.

"George, are you free?" He nearly jumped out of his
skin. Anne had come up the stairs and was standing
watching him. He had been oblivious of her presence,
as well as the group of students working quietly at the
end of the room.

He smiled and beckoned Anne over with a wave of
his hand. "Anne, you'd better see this, grab a chair, you
might need it. These," he patted the large folio, "were
in the roof. The builder found them."

Anne came over and touched the folio. "Oh George,

that's beautiful. I was going to ask you a question about the new database, but I think it can wait." She pulled up a chair and looked at the other books spread across the table top. "These were all in the roof?"

"Yes, it looks like they belonged to the cathedral. Okay. Let's have a look at this." He opened the large folio to the title page and they both looked in stunned silence at the engraving of William Shakespeare which stared back at them. It took them a full minute to read the title page and take in the details:

Mr William Shakespeares Comedies, Histories and Tragedies. Published according to the true Originall Copies.

The second impression. 1632.

"My good lord, what have you found?" said Anne. "That's incredible. And look, they missed out an apostrophe in his name."

George started laughing and found that he couldn't stop. Anne joined in and they sat there for several minutes, unsure what to say, just staring at the book.

"Well," said George, finally. "Do you think it's genuine? A second folio, is that right?"

"I think so," said Anne, taking a closer look. "I saw the first folio in the British Library last year, it's dated 1623. They said that without it, we would only have half of Shakespeare's plays. First folios are worth a fortune, there's only a few hundred of them left. I don't know about this second folio, but it looks in good condition." She turned over the page and whistled. "Sorry, should I be wearing gloves?"

"Don't worry," said George, "just be careful. I think

we need to pack it back up just as we found it and lock it away for now." He thought for a moment. "Anne, let's keep this between us for now. I'll call the British Library and see what they suggest."

"Right you are, Mum's the word."

"Thanks Anne. I think I'll call them right now."

The autumnal storm continued until Tuesday morning, soaking George on his way to work. He was drying his hair with a paper towel and turning on the reception computer when Mr Darcy walked in through the front door.

This was no dream. There in front of him was a tall gentleman dressed in an emerald-green tailcoat, cream breeches and long black boots. He had dark curly hair and the imperious expression known only to readers of *Pride and Prejudice*. It had to be Darcy. He walked up to the reception desk, bowed to George and placed an ivory envelope on the counter. He bowed again, turned and walked back out, closing the door smartly behind him.

George ran to the door, opened it and saw the man walking briskly across the square towards the shops. Returning to the library, he picked up the envelope. It was addressed in flowing handwriting as follows:

Mr and Mrs George Roosevelt
Whirligig Lane Subscription Library
Beaton

He opened the envelope and withdrew a white card with gold gilt edging.

Netherfield Ball

Mr Charles Bingley requests the pleasure of the company of Mr and Mrs George Roosevelt at Netherfield Park this Saturday evening at seven o'clock.

George grinned and jogged over to the door. He stood on the threshold, enjoying the fresh air and tapping the invitation card on his hand. A man in a bright yellow jacket was sweeping the wet autumn leaves into a pile. Out of the corner of his eye, a familiar figure was crossing the edge of the square towards the fruit shop on the corner. "Emily!" he shouted. Several people turned to look. Emily waved and came over, sweeping her blonde fringe back out of her eyes as the wind brushed the square.

"Hello George, everything okay?"

He smiled. "Yes, I just wondered if you have a couple of minutes, I have something very special to show you."

"Well, now I'm intrigued! I was just doing a little shopping, no hurry. Let's see."

George held the door open, took her trench coat and offered her a seat at the newspaper table.

"We found some books in the roof space. One in

particular is rather wonderful. Help yourself to a coffee,
I'll run up and fetch it."

From: Jules Martinez
To: George Sanders

George, I am so excited! Guess who walked into the library
this morning? Elizabeth Bennett!!

Sixteen

A knight at the library

George stared up at the face of Sir Isaac Newton, sat down on a stone bench and warmed his hands on his coffee. The huge statue stared serenely back at him, unperturbed by the bustle of the twenty-first century passing by.

Dr Rossi at the British Library had been very excited to hear from George and had asked him to come to London as soon as he could. The folio was nestling in his back pack, wrapped in a woollen throw.

He sipped his coffee and checked his watch. There was plenty of time before his four o'clock appointment. He looked up again at the statue, admiring the metallic gleam, the huge hands and the intense gaze. *Sir Isaac Newton. This sculpture embodies the purpose of the British Library as a place serving man's endless search for truth, both in the sciences and the humanities.* George nodded in salute to the statue and turned his gaze to the rest of the piazza.

His phone rang, it was Jules, on audio. "Hey George, did you make it to London on time?"

"Yes thanks Jules, just waiting outside the library, enjoying the view."

"So how do you like that statue, I think it's inspiring. Great place to sit, enjoying your coffee, just shooting the breeze."

"Absolutely ... how?" George looked up and saw a dark-haired woman in sunglasses waving at him from under a tree, about fifty yards away. "Jules? Is that you?" He jumped up and jogged over to meet her, his rucksack over one shoulder. They hugged, both laughing and looking at each other as if they hadn't spoken in months. "Goodness Jules, what are you doing here? It's brilliant to see you!"

"You too George, let's park here a minute." They sat on a bench and the sun made another brief appearance, lighting up the café, the white gazebos and the manicured lawns. The smell of freshly-baked croissants drifted across the piazza.

"Okay," said Jules, "so my friend Jennifer was coming over for a publishing conference in Bloomsbury. I told her you were coming to London on a special mission and she said why don't you tag along with me? It's only two days, and I thought, why not? I'm a little jet-lagged but here I am!"

"That's amazing, do you want to come in with me?"

"If I'm allowed. It is the British Library after all. Do I need a signed note from the President?" George laughed. "I think it'll be fine. If we have time afterwards, I'd love to show you the First Folio and the King's library."

"Sounds great George, count me in."

As they waited their conversation ebbed and flowed around Jennifer's conference, the folio and *Pride and Prejudice*. The clouds gradually drew over and a few drops of rain started to pitter-patter on the path. "Do you have an umbrella?" asked Jules. George reached into his back pack and produced one. "Of course you do, I bet you were a boy scout."

Sheltering under the umbrella, they made their way to reception and security where they met Dr Rossi. She led them through a labyrinth of corridors, down in a lift and finally they found themselves in a large brightly-lit room. She waved them in and invited them to sit at a long white counter which reminded George of a school laboratory bench. There were two large microscopes and a scanner which were placed rather incongruously next to some antique books with broken spines.

Dr Rossi was petite, her dark hair held back by a white comb. She smiled at them both. "First things first. Do you know the ownership of the folio?"

"Yes," said George, "at least, I believe that it originally belonged to the cathedral library. The cathedral donated most of their stock to our subscription library in the nineteen-seventies. I will need to talk to the Dean about the legal ownership and I have no idea how it came to be stored in the roof space."

"Okay," said Dr Rossi, "let's take a look."

George took off his back pack and unwrapped the bundle, finally revealing the dark-green calfskin cover of the folio with its gold-inscribed spine label: *Shakespeare's Plays*.

Jules gave a low whistle. Dr Rossi took the folio from George's hands and placed it carefully under the microscope. She spent several minutes examining the cover, the title page and the bindings.

"This certainly looks genuine," she said in a neutral tone, "but we will need to do some further checks. We would like to keep it for a couple of weeks if that's acceptable to you?"

"Of course," said George. "May I have a receipt?"

"Yes." Dr Rossi smiled and placed a hand on the cover. "Please don't worry, we'll take good care of it."

"So what's it worth then George?" They were standing next to the main gates to the British Library. The last of the afternoon sun cast a pale shadow of the iconic gate letters onto the red brick wall.

"I did a little research and it's certainly worth several hundred thousand pounds. If it's in tip top condition and the cathedral can provide some provenance, it could be worth up to half a million at auction." He watched as a bus purred to a halt next to them and a gaggle of chattering students stepped off.

"That's amazing George. Why aren't you more excited?"

He shrugged. "I have to reserve judgement. I just don't know how the cathedral authorities are going to react. They're usually pretty helpful, but they have their own ways and means. They may try to claim it back, in which case our library wouldn't make a penny."

"Okay, easy does it then. In the meantime, we may as well celebrate finding it. It could have been stuck in that roof for another century!"

"Absolutely, we should celebrate. Are you meeting Jennifer later? Could I gate-crash your dinner plans?"

"Of course George, I didn't come all this way to talk shop. We were hoping you wouldn't have to rush back."

"Great, where are we going?"

"Little French place in Bloomsbury. Virginia Woolf used to eat there."

"Sounds fabulous. By the way, how was Miss Elizabeth Bennett?"

"Awesome! My colleagues loved her too. She even stayed for photographs."

George grinned. "I can't imagine Mr Darcy doing that!"

Two hours later George, Jules and Jennifer were sitting in *Le Bon Viveur* brasserie, sharing a bottle of Pinot Noir and studying the menu.

"So how long have you guys known each other?" asked Jennifer. Her dark ringlets and angular glasses highlighted her high cheekbones. Jules looked at George and they both laughed. "Like forever," said Jules, "though I guess it's only what, fourteen years?"

"About that," said George, watching the candlelight play on their wine glasses. The black-and-white suited waiter had steered them graciously to a brown leather booth along the side wall of the restaurant. It was quiet this early in the evening.

"We met at Aberystwyth University in deepest, darkest Wales, would you believe," said George. "A winter conference for budding research librarians, straight after college."

"Wow, sounds like a blast," said Jennifer.

Jules put down her menu and took out her phone. "I have a picture, no laughing okay? Here you go, thirty librarians in a room, talking about how to stop students cheating in their essays."

"Very serious business, plagiarism," said George archly.

"We bonded over Jane Eyre, a shared passion for the Brontë sisters." Jules rolled her eyes and took a sip of wine.

"So," Jennifer hesitated, looking from George to Jules, "did you guys date?"

They laughed, the candlelight reflecting in their eyes. "No," said Jules, "we're friends. The best of friends." She raised her glass and they joined in the toast, their glasses ringing in the quiet of the restaurant.

After a delicious chicken casserole a la Normande, followed by caramel crème bruleé and coffee, Jennifer excused herself to call her boyfriend Rob. Jules looked across at George. "So did you tell Emily about the folio? How are things between you two?"

"I did, yes," said George, draining his glass and reaching for the bottle. "Actually I showed it to her. She thought it was amazing."

"And?"

"We're talking more. She came over for supper last week."

"That's good, right?"

"Yes. You know, the Jane Austen experience has been quite a distraction. In a good way."

"I agree. It's been great for us too, you know. I've been at the library every Saturday evening and Pat's been entertaining the kids. I'd call that a real home run!"

Standing outside the restaurant, they huddled into their coats and scarves, sheltering under the awning from the cool wind. "I should make a move," said George. "My train's around ten. It was lovely to meet you Jennifer, I look forward very much to reading your book." He kissed her chivalrously on the cheek and she blushed.

"You too George, you guys have been great company."

He turned to Jules and she stepped in for a bear hug. "Right then Jules. Or should I say Mrs Roosevelt? I still can't believe you're actually standing here. I shall see you on Saturday night at the Netherfield Ball."

Jules kissed him on the cheek. "I can't wait."

Seventeen

Pride and Prejudice

"You must learn some of my philosophy. Think only of the past as its remembrance gives you pleasure."

At a few minutes before midnight, George settled into the armchair on the second floor of the library and waited for the cathedral chimes. He placed the visor over his eyes and pictured Jules back in Maine, waiting for the final instalment.

"Good evening George."

He removed the visor and there in front of him was the translucent figure of Jane Austen.

"Miss Austen, I'm very glad to see you. I wanted to thank you for the opportunity to take part in your world. Jules and I are delighted that you chose us."

"Your pleasure is my satisfaction. I am pleased that you have enjoyed these little adventures into my novels.

Thank you for taking part with enthusiasm and respect. We would like to speak to you and Jules about your experience, perhaps next week?"

"Yes, of course."

"Thank you. We will contact you shortly. In *Pride and Prejudice*, we have included one small assignment only."

"Right. Will it be delivered on a card by a butler?"

Miss Austen smiled. "Perhaps. Goodbye George and good luck."

"Goodbye Miss Austen."

The white screen slowly faded away and George found himself inside a carriage. On the opposite seat sat Jules, wearing a long russet silk cloak, her dark hair swept back into the hood.

"Hey George, oh I like your evening dress!"

"Thank you ma'am, you look quite lovely yourself." George ran his fingers over the soft embroidered waistcoat, the silver fob watch and the dark breeches. The carriage rumbled forwards and the door was opened by a footman dressed in the elegant house uniform; a white wig and a royal-blue jacket with gold braiding. As they stepped from the coach onto the gravel path, George felt a touch on his left hand. Jules pointed towards the stone steps leading to the grand entrance to Netherfield Park. At the foot of the steps a group had gathered: five young women and an older couple. "The Bennetts," whispered Jules.

They moved slowly along the path, joining the other guests near the entrance. Watching and following the other ladies, Jules removed her cloak to reveal a flowing white muslin gown with an intricately embroidered bodice. George had time to appreciate the full splendour of their surroundings: the windows brightly lit by candelabras, liveried footmen carrying blazing torches, ladies in silk cloaks with ostrich feathers pluming above their heads.

As they stood atop the steps, George could see the receiving party, Mr Bingley and his sisters. In just a few moments they were announced and found themselves shaking hands with Mr Bingley. "So pleased to make your acquaintance Mr and Mrs Roosevelt. You are from the Americas we understand? Delighted that you could join us." Moving on, they stood to one side and watched as the last few guests came through the hall. A few feet to their left, two young ladies were also waiting. Mr Bingley walked briskly over to them, bowed and offered his arms to escort them into the ballroom. "That must be Jane and Elizabeth," George said quietly. Jane's fair hair was plaited at the back and decorated with chiffon and tiny flowers. Elizabeth Bennett's face glowed beneath her dark ringlets, her simple ivory dress perfectly contrasted with the lace ribbons and flower buds in her hair.

Jules sighed. "That is so beautiful, I could cry."

"Please don't," whispered George, "it's too early for tears."

The sound of violins floated from the ballroom and they followed the other guests through the double doors.

Evergreen swags framed the portraits and adorned the stage at the far end of the hall. Voices echoed from the walls as the candlelight flickered and reflected from every mirror and eye. George could almost smell the heady mix of lavender and orange blossom.

"What should we do?" asked Jules.

"Promenade I think," said George, offering his arm. They walked slowly around the edge of the room, weaving in and out of the happily-chatting guests, past the orchestra until they reached the fireplace where Jules pulled George to the side. "Mr Collins," she said, nodding her head in the direction of a soberly-dressed gentleman who was looking across the hall as if in search of someone. They watched as his gaze alighted on Elizabeth Bennett and Charlotte Lucas who were talking quietly near the entrance doors. The violins had stopped and couples were forming for the first dance. Showing an unlikely turn of pace, Mr Collins strode across the room, bowed to Elizabeth and held out his hand. "He has the first two dances," said Jules, standing on tiptoe to enjoy the amusement. There was plenty to be had. Mr Collins danced the wrong way, trod on Elizabeth's toe and at one point danced completely out of the set before Elizabeth could grab his hand and pull him back. "Over here Mr Collins!" she said with a forced smile.

George and Jules watched, laughed and clapped for the two dances until Elizabeth, clearly relieved, returned to talk to Charlotte.

A gentleman stepped in front of George and bowed. It was Mr Collins. "My dear sir," he said. "I understand from Sir William Lucas that you are intending to visit Rosings Park next month. I have the great honour and good fortune to know Lady Catherine de Bourgh; indeed she is my patroness for I am the clergyman of the parish."

"And what is your name sir?" asked George.

"I do beg your pardon, I should have asked Sir William to introduce us. My name is William Collins."

George smiled and gave a short bow and a quick wink at Jules. "I am very glad to make your acquaintance Mr Collins. I can assure you that *we* do not stand on ceremony. May I introduce my wife, Mrs Roosevelt?" Jules gave a little bob and stifled a giggle with her gloved hand.

"Mr and Mrs Roosevelt, I place myself entirely at your service if I am in residence when you make your tour of Rosings Park. Indeed I should very much like to show you around the gardens myself. Did you know that Rosings has no less than sixty-four windows?"

"So many," said George, raising his eyebrows. "I am very keen to see them all."

Mr Collins bent down to the floor and rose again with a card in his hand. He studied it for a second and then offered it to George. "Mr Roosevelt, I believe that you may have dropped this. Please excuse me; it is both my pleasure and my duty this evening to dance with more of my fair cousins." He bowed and walked away.

Jules finally gave way to a fit of giggles and they looked at the card. It said:

Mr and Mrs Roosevelt

The novels in which you have travelled have left a memory in Pride and Prejudice, one from each book. Your task is to find all six memories. Good luck.

George looked at Jules and shrugged. "What kind of memories? Any ideas?"

"Could be anything," said Jules. "Maybe music scores, fans, books, hats, I don't know." Her gaze swept the room for a moment. "Okay, how about we go our own way, check out the room and the entrance hall, meet back at the fireplace in ten minutes."

"Good plan Jules. See you shortly."

Jules walked slowly back to the entrance hall, looking closely at the paintings, window seats and side tables. George headed towards the musicians, wondering if there might be any familiar objects on the stage. He looked on the left and saw nothing promising. On the right hand side of the stage the players had stored their violin cases. Behind these was a wooden door. George tried the handle and the door opened to reveal a modest library with two long windows looking out onto the front gardens.

Standing in the middle of the room, he glanced around. There were no books left out on any surface; all was neat and tidy.

"Good evening sir" said a voice. George spun around to see a grey-haired gentleman with twinkling eyes and half-spectacles perched on his nose, seated in the corner. The man stood up and held out his hand. "Bennett's the name," he said, "I found this little haven of peace and quiet. You are Mr Roosevelt? I've been expecting you."

"I am delighted to meet you Mr Bennett. You found an escape here then?"

"Indeed I did. When one is so fortunate as to have one or two very silly daughters and a wife who embarrasses herself at every available opportunity, one does require an escape route."

"I saw your daughters Jane and Elizabeth," said George. "I believe that they are admired wherever they go."

"I am blessed indeed Mr Roosevelt, please do not mistake me. My wife and my daughters are as dear to me as life itself. A man should cherish his family, do you not agree?"

"Yes. Absolutely."

"Now, what is it you seek?"

"I'm looking for … I'm not sure what exactly. Maybe a couple of books."

"Well you are in the right place! I believe you will find two volumes in that bookcase, memories from two of your favourite novels."

In the dark wood bookcase next to the window, George found leather-bound volumes of selected poems by Pope and the novel *Tom Jones*. As he picked them up, a bell tinkled, as if it were time for dinner.

"There you are," said Mr Bennett. "Now, off you go and enjoy yourself. I will linger here as long as I may."

When George reached the fireplace Jules was already

there, looking over the crowd for him. "Any luck?" he asked.

"Piece of cake," she said, holding up a scroll. "It rang like a bell when I picked it up. They put it in the cloakroom in one of the fancy top hats."

"Excellent," said George, "that makes three!" He held up his two books. "These were in a little library next to the stage. I met Mr Bennett, he was very helpful. So what does the scroll say?"

"Just three words," said Jules, unrolling the parchment. The words "*negatron herb bay*" were written in large type across the middle. "I guess that's an anagram of Northanger Abbey."

"So it is. That was fairly straightforward. So *Mansfield Park* was next, if memory serves?"

"I won't forget that any time soon!"

"I remember now, the housekeeper, that ghastly Mrs Norris and the coming-out ball for Fanny Price."

"Okay," said Jules "so what is significant in the novel? The horse. Probably not! The play script, *Lovers Vows*, how about that?"

"Could be, I didn't see it in the library though," said George, looking around the ballroom. "I wonder. How about the amber cross William gave to Fanny, or the gold necklace. Where might they be hidden?"

"Not hidden. They could be right here in front of us. There's more gold than Fort Knox in this room, take a look around!"

"Okay, so I think the amber cross would be more distinctive. But how could we ask someone to lend it to us?"

"I think we'll find a way. You check out that end of the room, I'll do this." Once again they promenaded around the ballroom, this time trying to glance as innocently as possible at the jewellery worn by the ladies. After a minute, George noticed that Jules was in conversation with a red-coated officer near the stage. The officer was pointing back towards the entrance. George walked across just in time to hear the end of the conversation. "I found it over there," said the officer, "I would like to restore it to its owner as soon as possible for I imagine it to be a dear treasure."

"I'm sure you are right sir," said Jules. "May I look at it more closely?" He handed her a pretty amber cross on a short gold chain. A bell sounded. "Sir, I believe that I will be able to find the owner, if you will allow me?" He bowed his assent. "Thank you ma'am, I am most obliged to you."

Jules turned to George and they walked back to the fireplace. She placed the cross on the mantelpiece, together with the scroll. George added the two books. "Just two more then."

As they considered their next move, a young lady in an emerald-green dress approached them, pursued by the happily-smiling young officer. "Oh yes, my cross and chain! Thank you, thank you!" She gave a short curtsey to Jules, took the cross from the mantelpiece and the officer by the hand. Her eyes shone with tears. "I believe I must owe you a dance sir."

He bowed. "It would be my honour." The happy couple ran across and joined the next set.

George and Jules decided to try the hall, this time talking over their memories of *Emma*. They took a moment to enjoy the long sober family portraits and the red-gold autumn flowers. "Well," said George, "my memories of *Emma* are more of situations than objects as such. It could be a plate of strawberries I suppose, or the word games they play with letters, or …"

"Or the portrait of Harriet?" Jules was looking over his shoulder. "Turn around George."

He turned and they looked closely at the small portrait hanging on the wall which showed a young lady with fair hair wearing a simple Greek-style dress and standing in an arbour. Underneath was the inscription *Miss Harriet Smith*.

"Just look at that. Splendid." said George.

Jules held out her hand and touched the frame of painting. A bell tinkled. "I think that'll do it," she said laughing gently.

"Okay, one more to find. A memory of this evening."

Jules looked back towards the ballroom. "You know George, I'd like to talk to Lizzy and Charlotte. You go have some fun, I'll see you back here in ten." She made her way into the ballroom and placed herself near to Elizabeth and Charlotte, who were talking quietly. She removed one of her white lace gloves and dropped it innocently onto the floor. Charlotte noticed immediately, picked it up, smiled and offered it back to her.

"Oh thank you, I am so gauche, you are very kind. My name is Jules Roosevelt. I believe you are Miss

Bennett and Miss Lucas?"

They exchanged polite curtseys and enquiries before Jules decided that a direct question would be more fun. "Miss Bennett, are you acquainted with the tall gentleman who looks over at you?"

"Why yes, I am."

"And what is your opinion of his person and manners?"

"I … have not yet a proper impression of the gentleman; Mr Darcy I mean. Some say that he is excessively proud and superior. Mr Bingley and his sisters you know, would say the opposite."

"Miss Lucas, have you had the pleasure?"

"Only briefly," said Charlotte, looking across at Mr Darcy who was walking slowly in their direction. "I found his manners to be impeccable. Beyond that I could not say. I would only add that any young lady fortunate enough to gain his admiration would be a fool to ignore it. That kind of influence and standing is not easily to be found in the country."

Jules moved a little closer. "You tend towards the practical then, Miss Lucas, you are not excessively swayed by personality or romance?"

Charlotte smiled in amusement. "Most ladies of modest means do not have the luxury of bestowing their approval wherever they wish and denying it to those they dislike. We are *all* bound to be practical Mrs Roosevelt."

Jules nodded her agreement. "How right you are." Elizabeth now turned to her. "I have something for you Mrs Roosevelt … I believe you may need these shortly."

She handed Jules a pair of sky-blue ballet slippers and as she did, a bell tinkled. The slippers appeared, as if by magic, on Jules' feet.

Mr Darcy was approaching. Jules smiled her thanks, curtseyed and stepped away, staying just close enough to hear him ask Elizabeth to dance.

She looked around, saw George lingering by the door and beckoned him over. "Would you do me the honour of dancing the next with me? I have new shoes, you see?" George nodded happily and she led him over to the set.

The players finished the last with a glissando of violins and a hush came over the room. Elizabeth Bennett walked gracefully down the room, hand in hand with Mr Darcy.

"Why is everyone staring?" whispered George.

"Never mind, let's go and stand next to them."

"What?" George looked horrified.

"Come on George, let's go!" She reached for his hand and pulled him quickly down the hall. They came to the head of the dance and stood next to Darcy and Elizabeth. Jules looked across at George who was standing uncomfortably next to Darcy. The players began and the dancers moved down the line in formation, passing from arm to arm, then back again to their original positions. Once again, George found that he need not try to dance; his avatar moved for him. He had only to watch and enjoy.

The first dance ended and a slower, more processional movement began. Four dancers formed the front row, with Jules and George outside Darcy and

Elizabeth, holding hands. Thus began the conversation in which Elizabeth endeavoured to discover Darcy's character. George listened intently to the archly-phrased questions and enigmatic replies which passed back and forth between them. Darcy continued:

"What think you of books?" said he, smiling.

"Books – oh! no – I am sure we never read the same, or not with the same feelings."

"I am sorry you think so; but if that be the case, there can at least be no want of subject. We may compare our different opinions."

"No, I cannot talk of books in a ballroom; my head is always full of something else."

And so they continued, until Elizabeth acknowledged to Darcy that she could not make out his character *at all*.

The dance ended; they made their final bows as Elizabeth and Darcy separated.

Jules sighed. "I have danced with Mr Darcy. My life is complete."

"A dream fulfilled?" said George. "Perhaps that's what this experience has been?"

"Maybe not a dream, more like a time out of time."

"Mm, I see what you mean. I don't know if any other Saturday night will compare."

"Oh George, I'm sure you'll have plenty of great Saturday nights. Maybe not exactly like this of course!"

As they strolled back into the entrance hall, a green light appeared on the left next to a full-length portrait. Jules turned back to the ballroom. "Goodbye Lizzy," she murmured, "goodbye Darcy. We'll meet again soon."

"Ready?" said George, holding out his hand. Jules shook her head; her eyes were glistening. "Just give me a minute," she said, taking a last look at the ballroom. Then she took his hand. "Okay, time to go."

Eighteen

Enlightenment

Tuesday arrived with a blustery squall and a group of students from performing arts. One of the students, a tall dark-haired man looked rather familiar. The morning passed in a blur of dissertation advice, referencing and questions. In the afternoon the wind subsided and Anne took over the enquiry desk so that George could attend his meeting on the second floor with the Knightley Corporation.

He cautiously opened the door to the meeting room and looked around at the four faces which turned towards him. Two he had expected to see; two were strangers. "Hey, you must be George, great to meet you!" A broad-shouldered man with cropped hair jumped up, walked over and pumped his hand vigorously. "Jake Johnson, please call me Jake. This is my colleague Dylan Javernick." He gestured towards Dylan who was standing shyly by, wearing a grey *Stanford* hoody and fair curly hair. "Hey," he said casually, moving in to give George a light handshake.

"Let's sit down and start over with all those questions you must have. Drinks and cookies by the window, help yourself."

George filled his mug with black coffee and sat down next to Kamal who was seated at the far end of the table. Kamal smiled and shrugged. George leant over and shook his hand. "Well played Kamal," he said, laughing. On a large video screen on the end wall, Jules waved. "Hey George, good to see you." He waved back.

"It's a thrill to see you guys in person rather than on screen," said Jake. "I'm the product development manager at Art and I Tech. We're located not far from the Stanford campus. Dylan, maybe you could introduce yourself? Since you did most of the hard work." He grinned.

"Yeah," said Dylan, straightening up a little. "I'm Dylan Javernick from Knightley Corp. We're a small side shoot of Art and I Tech. So … we've been developing virtual reality engines which are aimed at the educational world rather than gaming. We chose Jane Austen because her books are popular the world over. It's been a real challenge getting the details right, but we think we did a pretty good job."

"Thanks Dylan," said Jake, "I think you nailed it, I really do. Anyhow, we asked a few people to help us out with the trial, including Kamal here who's been great. Thank you Kamal. The reason for today's meeting is first, to thank George and Jules for their fantastic role playing in the virtual world and to ask for their feedback. Second, to answer any questions you may have." Here he nodded to George and to Jules on the screen and opened his hands, inviting anyone to speak.

"Okay," said George, jumping in. "Maybe I can start, because I certainly have some questions. First of all, who is the voice of Jane Austen?"

Dylan raised a finger. "I can answer that. It may sound a little crazy but that voice is actually Jane Austen herself."

"Given that she's been dead for over two hundred years, that's quite an achievement," said George.

"Sure," said Dylan. "What we did was analyse all of her letters and writing, create a speech model and that's who you're talking to. It's not perfect, but we think it's a pretty good impression of how she would talk."

"It's very convincing," agreed George, "and combined with the hologram, it's incredibly lifelike."

"I can tell you about the hologram," said Kamal, standing up and walking to the drinks table. He picked up a lipstick-sized metal tube, clicked it and placed it back on the table. A few seconds later a hologram of Kamal in jeans and a t-shirt appeared next to him, as if an identical twin had joined him in the room.

"Wow, that is so tiny," said Jules, leaning into her screen to look more closely. "It's no wonder we couldn't see it."

"Very impressive," said George. "But why all the theatrics? If you'd asked us to take part in an official beta test, we would have been more than happy."

"Well," said Jake, "I was coming on to that. Dylan asked me if I knew any Jane Austen enthusiasts … " There was a knock at the door. It opened and a man walked in. It was Uncle Jack.

Jack smiled and raised his hand in greeting. "Sorry I'm late. Hi Georgie."

"Uncle Jack! What are you doing here?" George shot a confused look at Jack, who walked over and placed a hand on his shoulder.

"Hi Jack," said Jake. "We were just talking about the reasons for the drama and the … theatrics of our virtual world."

"Right, I'm sorry for all that cloak and dagger stuff Georgie." Jack walked over to the window and poured himself a coffee. "Me and Jake, we've known each other for a while; funny story, we met in Cuba whilst I was teaching there. Anyway, he asked me how you might feel about this, what are we calling it? The Jane Austen experience; I said absolutely, you'd love it. Only could we make it more fun. More like a proper adventure. I know you both have great imaginations, I thought you'd be really into it. We asked Kamal and Dylan, everyone agreed."

"Nobody asked me," said Jules from the screen. "It was amazing, really. Maybe not so ethical though."

Jake coughed and smiled broadly. "We, er made sure that the terms and conditions were clear, I think you remember? And Jack here was present in all the experiences to ensure fair play."

"Fair play?" said George, turning to Jack. "What part did you actually play?"

"Okay, they needed a role playing person to give you the clues. I played the butlers and the clue-givers. They fixed me up with a computer rig that I could use anywhere." He paused to give this information time to sink in. From the screen Jules started laughing. "Oh that's hilarious, you were the butler! Wait a minute, you tried to kiss me, you ass!" Jack grinned sheepishly and held up his hands in surrender. "You got me, I did. But it was only virtual, not real, okay? Just for research."

"It felt pretty real at the time, I can tell you," said Jules. "But I'll forgive you. One time only."

"I tried to punch you in Sense and Sensibility!" said George, still feeling somewhat aggrieved that he had been blindsided by Jack's games.

"You did Georgie, but admit it, you enjoyed it as much as I did."

George sat back in his chair and shrugged. "I did, yes. It was exciting, of course it was. Do you have any more bombshells for us Jack?"

"No," said Jack, "that's it for me."

"I have another question," said Jules, "for Dylan. I've tried a few virtual realities but I've never seen that kind of detail on the faces of the avatars. I mean, I cried and so did my avatar. I could feel the tears with my gloved hands, it was amazing."

"Thanks," said Dylan, "that's what we were shooting for. We worked with another start-up on the haptic gloves. Those guys were brilliant. You could feel a cold wind, tears on your face or the glass on the surface of a watch, just through the gloves. We've been working on the avatar faces and expressions for over two years so they could mirror what you're feeling."

"What happened in Mansfield Park?" asked George.

"Oh, sorry about that, it was just a glitch. The whole program froze. It was useful though, we found a few bugs."

"I thought the whole project ran super smooth," said Jake. "Dylan, do you want to talk about the next steps in testing?"

"Just a minute," said George, "before you come on to that. Who were Darcy and Elizabeth when they delivered our invitations?"

"They were actors," said Kamal, "from performing arts."

"Ah," said George, nodding, "you can tell them that they played their parts beautifully. Put them up for an Oscar."

"Happy to."

"Okay … in terms of roll-out," said Dylan, "we'll do some more official testing with a range of people, different ages and so on. The great thing is we know what works best. We think playing as extra characters, the Roosevelts in your case worked out really well. We weren't so happy with *Emma* where you played a scene as a major character. That only works if you're an Austen superfan." He nodded to George and to Jules on the screen. "That could be an add-on for actors maybe. Anyhow, we want to sell it to schools and universities worldwide, that's the target market."

George looked across at Dylan. "I would bear in mind that this only works well if you've read the books. Otherwise it would be just a costume drama in virtual reality."

"Fair point." said Dylan. "If it's okay with you guys, could we have a follow-up talk over the details?"

"Fine by me," said Jules. "George?"

"No problem. And Dylan, would you pass on our thanks to your team? Although I feel rather like a guinea-pig, I have had a brilliant time."

"Me too!" said Jules, giving a thumbs-up. Dylan nodded, looking pleased. "Sure, thanks."

Jake placed his hands flat on the table. "Okay, I'm sure that we all have plenty to chew over, so let's break it up and talk it out."

Dylan walked over to talk to Kamal whilst George turned to Jack. "You sneaky old git," he said playfully, "I would try and hit you again, but I expect you'd dodge it."

"Yup, I would. We had a laugh though didn't we Georgie? How about you Jules?"

"You're a very naughty man Jack. But yeah, we did."

Nineteen

Money talks

"Good luck George," said Roxie, "I hope it works out, for all of us, you know?"

"Thanks Roxie. I hope we won't be packing our bags and books any time soon, but you never know."

"Hope for the best and prepare for the apocalypse, that's what I always say," said Jim. He was sitting on the sofas next to Roxie, skim-reading the newspaper.

Anne came up the stairs looking apprehensive. She was even wearing plain black shoes. George put on his tweed jacket and picked up a manila folder from his desk. He knew that the Professor saw a very different future for the library, but he was prepared to stand up for their own vision. "Ready Anne?"

"Ready as I'll ever be."

"Try not to worry," said George. "We have a good argument and plenty of evidence."

"Will they listen though?"

"Perhaps." He turned to Roxie and Jim. "Will we see you both on Saturday at Sylvie's?"

"We wouldn't miss it," said Roxie, looking at Jim, who nodded enthusiastically.

"Great, see you there."

George and Anne knocked and walked into the small meeting room for their funding update with the Professor. He was standing at the window watching the trees as the afternoon light began to fade into grey.

"Hello, hello, sit down, please." He sounded chirpy and optimistic. "As you know, we have a trustees meeting next week, so this is a chance to look again at the finances and put together our proposals for the board." He paused. George and Anne were silent.

"Right, well I'll begin then. We have received some limited proposals for increasing income, but none sufficient to bridge the gap in the finances. You will have seen my summary. I am therefore proposing to the board that we sell the building and lease back one floor for a smaller library. There will be a vote, of course."

Anne stared silently at her feet. George looked the Professor straight in the eyes. "What about the books?"

"The books, yes." The Professor sucked in his mouth and looked at a faded landscape canvas on the wall. "Some could be retained in the smaller space. The rest would need to be … " he waved his hand, "moved on."

"The staff?"

"That would be a matter for discussion. We hope

that the permanent staff could be retained."

George stood up and walked to the window. "Professor, we would like the trustees to consider an alternative approach. You may not be aware that we found some first editions in the roof space and a second folio of Shakespeare's plays. They belonged to the old cathedral library."

"You found a second folio in the roof? How did it get there?" The Professor looked incredulous.

"We don't know. It's currently with the British Library and they have confirmed that it's genuine. I'll forward you their notes."

"How much is it worth? Could we sell it?"

"We don't own it."

"Well that's a disappointment."

"Yes and no. I've had some discussions with the Dean of the cathedral. They are willing to share ownership of the books. In fact, they would like to open a new exhibition of the cathedral's treasures, to include the second folio. Our library would share some of the income."

"That is good news George, but I don't imagine this would cover our annual losses. Do you?"

"On its own, no." He sat back down. "We do have some other sources of income. Anne, could you tell the Professor about the grants please?"

Anne took a sheet from George's folder and placed it on the desk. "This is a brief summary of two grants which the library have secured in principle. The first you're aware of; it's a sum to protect the roof space for the barbastelle bats and to allow access for educational

189

work by Natural England." She took another sheet from the folder and pushed it across the desk.

"This is the second grant. It's a provisional award of twenty thousand pounds a year for three years for the promotion of literacy in the community. We'll be the only library in Beaton with this status and would offer free membership to every child in the city. There would be holiday clubs to encourage reading and we would look to engage local schools. We could even have guest teachers in the hologram room, Einstein, Mozart, maybe even Jane Austen." The Professor gave a wry smile at this.

"We have more ideas," said George, "but we need to know that the Trustees will back the library for at least three years."

The Professor turned in his chair, took off his glasses and rubbed them absent-mindedly on his striped shirt. Turning back towards them, he appeared to have come to a decision.

"Thank you for your time and efforts in preparing these." He picked up the papers from the desk. "I don't know if it will make a difference, we'll have to look at the numbers."

"Thanks," said George. "In the meantime, I've spoken to the other five trustees to canvas their opinions."

"You've gone to them behind my back?" The Professor's bonhomie had evaporated.

"I prefer to call it consultation," said George.

The Professor was silent for a moment, then he stacked his papers and stood up. "I think we're done here," he said and walked out of the room without another word.

Twenty

Love and friendship

A bright spotlight picked out the piano player on the stage, absorbed in a free-form melody over *What is this thing called love*. The drummer and bass player maintained a slow, steady rhythm. Kamal was perched on a stool, holding his guitar ready, nodding his head and watching the others play.

Kamal had invited all of his colleagues and friends to join them for Saturday jazz night. *Sylvie's* was nearly full, the tables and booths humming with conversation. George was sitting with Anne, Roxie, Jim and Poppy at a round table in the corner.

"That was quite a gamble George," said Roxie, sipping her rum old fashioned and twirling the ice in the glass.

"It was," acknowledged George, "but sometimes you have to throw caution to the four winds and see how it lands."

Roxie nodded. Poppy leant into the table. "The Professor resigned? Just like that?" She shook out her dark curls in disbelief and smiled.

"He did," said George. "He came in yesterday and shook my hand. I was surprised. *He* had a vision of the building as a commercial centre with a small library. We didn't share his ideas and, as it turned out, neither did all the trustees. He behaved in quite a gentleman-like manner actually. He said that he felt it was time for someone else to take over at the helm. That was it, no hard feelings."

"Thank goodness for that," said Anne, raising her glass.

"It's a relief, certainly, but quite a challenge too" said George. "But I think we can raise our game, don't you Anne?"

"Yes I do. Bring it on!"

"Well I couldn't imagine this place without our library," said Roxie. "I don't like the public library rooms, too modern, too noisy."

"We may have to put up with a little noise," said Anne, "but it's all in good cause."

"Amen to that," said Jim, lifting his beer glass and admiring the pale blonde colour. "This is great George, what is it?"

"Organic real ale," said George, "it's a favourite around here. You can smell the acorns. Cheers everyone!" They raised their glasses and Roxie stood up. "I would like to propose a toast to Jane Austen," she said. "I can't believe you've been spending every Saturday night gallivanting around in the nineteenth century. I'm quite jealous."

"Well Roxie, you may be able to join in next year if they launch it. Ask Kamal, he might give you a sneak preview."

"It's great that the bats are safe," said Jim, "you don't know how much it means to us. If you ever need anyone to do some bat tours, let me know. You might need to put in proper floor though; don't want to put my foot in it, if you know what I mean."

"We're already on it," said Anne, "the grant, you remember? I think we'll have the best looking bat house in the country!"

Everyone laughed and Anne slipped away to catch up with Handsome Raj as he stood at the bar. The band started playing *A case of you* and a few couples took to the dance floor in front of the stage. Raj came over to join them and stood chatting comfortably to Anne and Poppy. Out of the corner of his eye, George saw the door open. Emily slipped in quietly and looked around.

"I'm so glad you could come." George took Emily's coat and they threaded their way through the tables back to the corner. "Drink?"

"I would love a coffee," said Emily, pulling off her beret and smoothing back her hair. She waved to Anne and Roxie. "Hello everyone." George made the introductions, Roxie ordered the drinks and Kamal came over as the band took a break.

"So Kamal," said Roxie, "how did you keep the

secret for six weeks?"

Kamal grinned. "No problem really. I just had to haunt the library like a poltergeist every Saturday night. It was a hoot!" One of his bandmates tapped him on the shoulder as he headed back to the stage. "Sorry guys," said Kamal, "we're back on, I'll see you later." He ran off to fetch his guitar.

Roxie took Jim's hand and pulled him to his feet. "You're having a dance with me, ready or not," she said. Jim gave a lopsided smile and nodded. "If you say so."

"George?" said Emily. "Would you like to dance?"

"Oh … yes," said George, "yes I would."

They joined Roxie and Jim on the dancefloor, moving slowly to the bossa nova syncopation of *The girl from Ipanema*.

An hour later, Emily looked at her phone and whispered in George's ear. He nodded and she reached for her coat, waving goodbye to the others. The band finished up with *Between the devil and the deep blue sea* and a grateful audience applauded loudly as they took their bows.

The Sunday evensong bells rang out from the cathedral as a soft rain washed the twilight greens. George stood at the balcony window and watched as Squawk settled on the rail and twitched his tail feathers. "You're back then, where have you been?" The magpie raised its head nonchalantly and hopped across to the other rail. "You're a funny little fellow, but I like you," said

George. "Tell you what, I'll introduce you to Emily later." He moved back inside and stood in front of the mirror, adjusting a royal-blue bowtie.

"You look very smart sir."

"Thank you Bertie."

"Dinner is served in thirty minutes sir."

"Right you are Bertie. By the way, would you like to call me George, rather than sir? I feel like you're one of the family now."

"I would like that sir. *George*."

"Excellent. Could you call Jules please? On the large screen."

The highland glen dissolved and Jules appeared on screen, sitting on her sofa in a simple black dress. "Looking sharp George. Wow, is that a bow tie?"

"Indeed it is. You look all ready for cocktails."

Jules was holding a small parcel wrapped in pale yellow tissue paper. "I've got mine, do you have yours?" she said, holding up the parcel.

"Right here." George picked up a small white box from the coffee table and sat in the armchair facing the screen.

"Okay, on three," said Jules, laughing. "One, two, three." She unwrapped her package and George lifted the lid on the little box. Inside was a small book bound in grained red leather; *The works of Alexander Pope*. He looked up at the screen. "My goodness, Jules, that is lovely, thank you."

Jules removed the last piece of tissue paper from her present. It revealed a small cloth-bound volume in sky blue with a cover drawing of tiny oak trees: *Walt*

Whitman, Leaves of grass. "Oh George, you remembered, thank you." She put her hand to her cheek and smiled back at the screen. "I told you my old copy had fallen apart and you remembered. This is ... really beautiful. Okay, take a look inside your book. Mr Pope wrote you a line"

George opened the book at the title page. Under the author's name Jules had written. *"To err is human, to forgive, divine."* He was silent for a moment and felt his eyes grow warm. A tear fell onto his cheek and he wiped it gently away.

"George, are you crying? After all this time?"

He looked away and then turned back, trying to find his voice. "No ... I'm just. I don't know what to say."

"It's okay, I cry all the time. You should try it, it's good for you. Those are tears of happiness aren't they?"

"Yes," said George, recovering his composure, "yes they are."

Emily walked into the room and placed a vase of yellow roses on the dining table. "Hello Jules," she said, "where are you off to later?"

"Emily, great to see you. Pat's booked our favourite place down on the wharf. There's a crazy northeaster blowing off the gulf so we won't be out on the deck."

"I hope you have a great time," said Emily.

"Thanks. So George, have you booked your flight for the spring yet?"

"Yes, all arranged. But is the New England Brontë convention ready for *us* Jules?"

"They'd better be! I heard it's the best Brontë convention in the country. You know I'm going to miss those Saturday night adventures of ours."

"So am I. We'll have to arrange a film night or something."

"Count me in. No regency dramas though."

"Agreed, all new adventures."

Jules looked around as her door chimed. "Okay George, I have to go."

"Thanks Jules. For everything."

"Take care George."

The screen returned to the glen.

"Bertie, play Chopin's *Nocturne* please."

The opening notes echoed in the silence. George watched as Emily moved around the table, placing the wine glasses and lighting a tall candle. She noticed him, turned and smiled. "Chopin?"

"I thought it was time for a change. It's been a Chopin kind of day."

"So it has."

"Perhaps we need a fresh soundtrack for our new memories."

"I like that. Are you ready for dinner?"

"Thank you. I'm on my way."

Acknowledgements

My thanks to you, dear reader, I hope you enjoyed the book.

To family and friends for love and support. Jane, Jamie and Peter. Alan and Jill (Mum and Dad), Paul, Sonia and Jeremy. Will, Diane, Martin, Helen and those who helped with suggestions and proofreading.

To the lovely librarians, you know who you are.

and finally ... to Jane Austen, for inviting us into her world.

Printed in Great Britain
by Amazon

64124639R00121